D0456964

CONTENTS

Part One

1946

I

MAMMA IN FRONT; ME BEHIND. MAMMA STRIDES through the narrow streets in the Spanish Quarter: it takes two steps of mine to keep up with every one of hers. I look at people's shoes. Shoes with no holes in them equal one point; shoes with holes in them, minus one point. No shoes: zero points. New shoes: I get a star-studded prize. I've never had a pair of shoes of my own; I wear other people's shoes and they always hurt. Mamma says I don't walk straight but it's not my fault; it's other people's shoes that are the problem. They are the shape of the feet that wore them before me. They've taken on their habits, walked on other streets, played other games. By the time they get to me, what do they know about the way I walk, or where I want to go? They need to get used to me little by little; but then my feet grow, the shoes get too small for me, and we're back to square one.

Mamma in front; me behind. I have no idea where we're going, she says it's for my own good. There must be a catch, like when

I had head lice. It's for your own good, she said, and then she shaved my head so I looked like a melon. Luckily, my friend Tommasino got the melon treatment, too, for his own good, of course. The kids in our street teased us, saying we looked like skulls that had escaped from the ossuary at Fontanelle Cemetery. In the beginning, Tommasino wasn't my friend. One day, I saw him steal an apple from Capajanca, the vegetable man with the barrow at Piazza del Mercato, and I thought we could never be friends because Mamma Antonietta always says we may be poor, but we are certainly not thieves. Better beggars than thieves. But Tommasino had seen me and had taken an apple for me, too. Since the apple had been given to me, and it wasn't me who stole it, I finished it off. I was so hungry he could see it in my eyes. We've been friends since then. Apple friends.

Mamma walks right in the middle of the street and never looks down. I drag my feet and count points so I don't get scared. I count up to ten on my fingers and then I start again. When I get to ten times ten, something nice will happen. That's how the game goes. Until now nothing nice has ever happened to me, though. Maybe I count the points wrong. I like numbers quite a lot. Letters not so much. One by one, I can recognize them, but when they're all mixed up into words, I get confused. Mamma says she doesn't want me to grow up like she did, and that's why she sent me to school. I went, but I didn't like it one bit. For one thing, the kids were yelling all day and I used to come home with a headache. The classroom was tiny and smelled like sweaty feet. And then I had to sit still all day at my desk in silence and draw rows and rows of straight lines. Our teacher had a pointy chin and spoke with a lisp. If anyone copied her, she would whack them on the head. I had ten whacks in five days. I counted them like my shoe points, and I didn't get a prize that time either. After a while, I decided I didn't want to go to school anymore.

Mamma wasn't happy about it, but she said at least I had to learn a trade and so she sent me to collect rags. At first, I liked it. My job was to go from house to house, or down to the garbage dump, pick up old rags, and then take them to Capa 'e Fierro's market stall. After a few days, I was so tired from my rounds that I even missed the whacks the pointy-chinned teacher had given me.

Mamma stops in front of a gray-and-red building with big windows.

"It's here," she says.

This school looks nicer than the last one. It's quiet inside and there's no stench of feet. We go up to the second floor, and they make us sit on a wooden bench in a corridor, until a voice calls out: "Next." Since nobody else moves, Mamma thinks we must be next and we go in.

Mamma's name is Antonietta Speranza. The signorina waiting for us writes her name on a sheet of paper and says, "This is your last option." That's when I think: Okay, Mamma's going to turn around and go home now. But she doesn't move.

"Do you whack your students?" I ask the signorina, covering my head with my arms just in case. She laughs and pinches my cheek gently, without squeezing.

"Sit down," she says, and we sit down facing her.

The signorina doesn't look a bit like my last teacher. She doesn't stick her chin out, her smile is full of straight white teeth, her hair is cut short, and she wears pants like a man. We sit in silence. She says her name is Maddalena Criscuolo and that maybe Mamma remembers her, because she fought to liberate us from the oppression of the Nazi-Fascists. Mamma nods her head, but I can tell that she has never heard the name Maddalena Criscuolo before today. Maddalena tells us that during the "Four Days of Naples" she had saved the bridge at Rione Sanità, because the Germans wanted to blow it up with dynamite; in the end, she says, she was given a bronze medal and a certificate. I think she would have done better with a pair of new shoes, because she has one good shoe and one with a hole in it (zero points). She says we have done the right thing coming to see her, that most people are too ashamed, that she and her comrades knocked on every single door in the neighborhood to convince mothers that this was a good thing, for them and for their children. She also says that they had a lot of doors slammed in their faces, and a few curses too. I can believe it because when I go and knock on doors looking for old rags, people often cuss at me. The signorina says that a lot of good families have trusted them, that Mamma Antonietta is a brave woman, and that she is giving an important gift to her son. I've never had a gift, except for an old tin sewing box I keep my precious things in.

Mamma Antonietta waits for Maddalena to stop talking, because talking is not her strong point. The woman says kids should be given a chance but, to tell the truth, I would be much happier with a slice of bread with ricotta cheese and sugar on top. I tried it once at a party I crashed with Tommasino, held by some Americans (old shoes: minus one point).

Mamma doesn't say a word, that's why Maddalena keeps talking: they've organized some special trains to take children up north. My mother finally says something.

"Are you sure you want him? Look at this kid. He was sent by God to punish us!"

Maddalena says they'll put a whole bunch of us on the train, not just me.

So it's not a school, I finally realize, smiling.

Mamma isn't smiling.

"If I had a choice, I wouldn't be here. This is my only choice, so see what you can do."

When we leave, Mamma walks one step ahead of me, but more slowly than before. We walk by the pizza stall, where normally I would be pulling on her skirt and wailing until she walloped me. This time, though, she stops.

"Pork rind and ricotta cheese, please," she asks the boy behind the counter. "Just one."

I hadn't asked her for anything, and I realize that if Mamma, of her own accord, decides to buy me fried pizza for a mid-morning snack, there must be a catch somewhere.

The man wraps a piece of pizza as yellow as the sun and as wide as my face. I'm so scared I'll drop it that I grab on to it using both hands. It's warm and smells delicious; I blow on it and the aroma of olive oil fills my nose and mouth. Mamma bends down and looks me in the eye.

"You heard what she said, right? You're a big boy now; you'll be eight soon. You know the situation we're in, don't you?"

She wipes the grease off my face with the back of her hand.

"Come on, let me have a taste," she says, twisting off a corner of the dough with her fingers. Then she straightens up and starts for home. I don't ask her anything and set off after her. Mamma in front; me behind.

2

MADDALENA DIDN'T COME UP IN CONVERSA-
tion again. I thought Mamma must have forgotten or
changed her mind. But then, a few days later, a nun came to the
house, sent by Padre Gennaro. The nun knocked at the door and
Mamma peeked out the window and said: "Now what does this
penguin want?"

The sister knocked again, so Mamma put her sewing down and
opened the door a crack, so the nun could only get her face in. It was
all yellow. The nun asked if she could come in, and Mamma opened
the door a little wider, but you could see she really didn't want her
there. The nun said Mamma was a good Christian and Our Lord
sees everything and His creatures do not belong to their mothers
or their fathers; they are all God's children and, anyway, the poli-
ticians want to send us all to Russia, where we'll all be killed and
nobody will ever make it back home. Mamma didn't say a word.
She's really good at keeping quiet. After a while, the nun was bored
and left. So I asked Mamma: "Do you really want to send me to

Russia?" She picked up her sewing again and started muttering to herself: "What Russia? Russia, huh? . . . I'd like to see that sister on her own with a child . . . it's easy to talk when you don't have kids of your own. Where was that penguin when my Luigino fell ill, eh?"

Luigi would have been my big brother if he hadn't gotten bronchial asthma as soon as he came into the world. In any case, by the time I came along, I was already an only child.

"Fascists, Communists, they're the same to me; just like priests and bishops," Mamma went on, because she doesn't talk much to other people, but she does talk to herself quite a bit. "Up till now, it's been nothing but hunger and hard work for me . . ."

If my big brother hadn't had the bad idea of getting bronchial asthma, he would now be three years older than me. Mamma hardly ever says his name but she keeps a picture of him on her bedside table with a little red light in front of it. Zandragliona, the nice lady who lives in the ground-floor apartment right in front of ours, told me about it. She says Mamma was so sad, they didn't think she would ever get over it. But then she gave birth to me, and she was happy again. Well, I don't make her happy like he did. Otherwise, she wouldn't be sending me to Russia.

I decide to go to see Zandragliona. She knows everything, and even if she doesn't, she knows how to make it up. Zandragliona says they're not taking me to Russia. She says that she knows Maddalena Criscuolo and that those women we saw want to help us; they want to give us hope. Well, I've got "hope" in my name because I'm called Speranza like Mamma Antonietta. My first name is Amerigo. Mamma said my father chose my name. I've never met him, and every time I ask Mamma, she rolls her eyes like it's about to rain and she hasn't had time to bring the washing in. She says he's a truly great man. I think he must have gone to America to seek his fortune. "Will he ever come back?" I ask. "Sooner or later," she answers. "I hope so," I say. Well, that's all he left me. My name. I suppose that's something.

Since the news of the children's train transports came out, the neighborhood is abuzz. Each person says something different: they'll sell us and send us to America to work; they'll take us to Russia and gas us; the bad kids will be sent off and the good ones will get to stay. Some don't give a damn and carry on as if nothing is happening, because they are total ignoramuses. I'm ignorant, too, though in the neighborhood they call me "Nobèl" because I know so much. And because I talk a lot. I go around town. I hear stories. I stick my nose into other people's business. No one is born knowing everything.

Mamma Antonietta doesn't want me talking about her business. In fact, I don't tell anyone that Capa 'e Fierro, Iron Head, has stashed packets of coffee under our bed. Nor do I say that Capa 'e Fierro comes to our house and locks himself in with Mamma. I wonder what he tells his wife? Maybe that he's playing pool. He sends me out when he comes. He says he and Mamma need to get down to work. So I go out and look for stuff: rags, remnants, clothes American soldiers have thrown away, dirty tatters full of fleas. When he first started coming to the house, I didn't want to leave them alone there. I didn't like Capa 'e Fierro acting like he was head of the family. But Mamma said I had to show respect, because he helps put food on our plates and, anyhow, he knows people in important places. She said he's a good salesman and that I should learn from him. That he could be my guide. I didn't answer her, but since then, whenever he comes, I go out. Whatever scraps I bring back home, Mamma has to scrub, clean, and mend, and then we take them to Capa 'e Fierro, who has a stall at Piazza del Mercato. Every now and again, he manages to sell something to people a little less poor than us. In the meantime, I look at everyone's shoes and count up the points on my fingers. When I get to ten times ten, something nice will happen: my father will come back from America, and I will be the one to throw Capa 'e Fierro out of the house, not the other way around.

Once the game actually worked, though. In front of the San Carlo Theater, I saw a man with such shiny, brand-new shoes that it earned me a hundred points straight off. And then, when I went home, Capa 'e Fierro was outside the door. Mamma had seen his wife on the Corso with a new handbag on her arm. Capa 'e Fierro said, "You have to learn to wait. If you wait, your time will come." But Mamma said, "Today, you can wait," and she didn't let him in. Capa 'e Fierro lit a cigarette and walked away, his hands in his pockets. I followed him because it gave me a kick to see him disappointed. I called out to him.

"No work today, Capa 'e Fierro? Is it a holiday?"

He turned around and squatted down in front of me. He pulled on his cigarette and then blew little smoke circles into my face.

"Well, young man. Women and wine are the same. Either you dominate them, or they dominate you. If you let them dominate you, you go crazy. You are a slave to them. I've always been free and I always will be. Come. Let's go to the osteria. Today, I'm going to introduce you to red wine. Today Capa 'e Fierro is going to make a man out of you!"

"Pity I can't oblige you, Capa 'e Fierro," I said. "I have things to do."

"What could you possibly have to do, young man?"

"I have to go and look for rags, as usual. They're worth nothing, but at least they put food on the table. Please excuse me."

I left him there, the smoke rings vanishing into the air.

I put whatever rags I can collect into a basket Mamma gave me. Because the basket gets heavy when it fills up, I started balancing it on my head like I'd seen women do at the market. But carry it today, carry it tomorrow, my hair started falling out and I ended up with a bald patch on my head. That's why she shaved my head, and I looked like a melon. It wasn't head lice!

During my scavenging, I ask around whether anyone knows about the trains but nobody does. Tommasino says he's not going, because they have everything they need at home, and his mother, Donna Armida, lacks for nothing. Severe Pachiochia, who commands a lot of respect in our neighborhood, says that these things didn't use to happen when there was still a king in Italy; mothers didn't use to sell their children. She says that these days there's no longer any *dig-ni-ty*, and every time she says it like that, you can see her brown gums, as she clenches the few yellow teeth she has left in her mouth, and spits through the gaps. I think Pachiochia must have been born ugly, and that's why she never found a husband, but we're not allowed to say anything about this because it's her weak point. That and the fact that she doesn't have any kids. She once kept a little goldfinch, but it flew away. We're not supposed to talk about the goldfinch either.

Zandragliona also never married. She's still a signorina. Nobody knows why. Some people say she couldn't decide among her many suitors and ended up on her own. Everyone says she's quite rich and doesn't want to share her money. Some say she once had a fiancé but he died. Or that she had a fiancé, but then she found out he was married. I say they're all gossips.

Only once did Pachiochia and Zandragliona agree on something. That was when the Germans came all the way up to our street looking for something to eat, and our two neighbors put pigeon poop in the *casatiello* pie saying it was pork rind, which is a specialty of ours. The soldiers wolfed it down and said *gut, gut!* to Pachiochia and Zandragliona, who were poking each other in glee and laughing in their sleeves. We never saw the soldiers again, and there was never any punishment.

MAMMA ANTONIETTA HASN'T SOLD ME. NOT YET, anyway. But then, a couple of days later, I came home with my basket of rags and found Maddalena Criscuolo at the house. I said to myself: "Here we are. They've come to buy me, too!" So, while Mamma is talking to the lady, I'm spinning around the room like I'm half-crazy or something, and whenever they ask me anything, I either don't answer or I stammer and dribble on purpose. I'm trying to look like I'm brain-damaged so they won't want to buy me anymore. Who would be so dumb as to buy a cripple or a stutterer, huh?

Maddalena says she came from a poor family, too, and she isn't well-off even now. Being hungry isn't anything to be ashamed of, she says; it's an injustice, and women should unite to make things better. Pachiochia says that if all girls cut their hair short and wore pants like Maddalena then the world would go to hell in a handbasket. I say she shouldn't talk because she's the one with a mustache! Maddalena doesn't have a mustache. She has a lovely red mouth and white teeth.

Maddalena lowers her voice and says she knows Mamma's story. She knows how she suffered for her tragedy, and says women should help one another. She calls it solidarity. Mamma Antonietta stares at a point on the wall, where there is nothing to look at, for two minutes, and I know she's thinking about my big brother, Luigino.

Before Maddalena, there were other ladies coming to the house, but they didn't have short hair and they didn't wear pants. They were real signoras with smart clothes and that blond fresh-from-the-hairdresser look. When they came into our street, Zandragliona would always make a face and say: "Here come the charity dames." At the beginning, we were happy because they brought us food packages, but then, when we opened them, we saw there was no pasta, no meat, no cheese, no nothing. There was rice. Always rice. Nothing but rice. When they came, Mamma would look up at the sky, as if a storm was coming and we were only halfway home, and say: "We'll kill ourselves laughing to-night with another risible risotto!" The charity dames didn't get it, but when they realized that nobody wanted the food pack-ages, they said the rice was "Made in Italy" and they were work-ing to promote it. After a while, people stopped opening their doors to them when they knocked. Pachiochia says we know no gratitude, we deserve nothing, and there's no longer any *dig-ni-ty*. Zandragliona says the dames come to gloat. Them and their rice. Anytime someone gives away something useless, she says: "The charity dames are here!"

Maddalena promises we'll have fun on the train, and that the families up north will treat us like their own children. They'll take care of us and give us food and new clothes and shoes (two points). I stop my crippled dribbling act when I hear this and say: "Mamma! Sell me to this lady!" Maddalena's big red mouth opens wide into a laugh, just as Mamma gives me a clout around the ear with the back of her hand. I put my hands up to my face; I don't know whether it's burning more from the smack or more from my shame. Maddalena stops laughing and reaches out to touch Mamma's arm. Mamma pulls away, as if she'd touched a boiling hot pan. She doesn't like being touched or even stroked. Then Maddalena speaks in a serious voice and says that she doesn't want to buy me. The Party is organizing something that has never been undertaken before, that will make history, and that people will remember for years to come. "You mean, like the pigeon poop in the *casatiello*?" I ask her. Mamma Antonietta looks at me, and I look at her. It feels like another spank is on its way but, instead, she says: "And you? What do you want to do?" I say that if they actually give me a pair of brand-new shoes (a star-studded prize), I'll go up north to the Communists like a shot, on foot if necessary. Maddalena smiles while Mamma's head moves up and down, which I know means I'm in.

3

MAMMA ANTONIETTA STOPS IN FRONT OF THE door where the Communists have their headquarters in Via Medina. Maddalena told us we had to put our name down on the list for the children's train. On the first floor, there are three young men and two signorinas. As soon as the signorinas see us, they lead us into a room where there is a desk with a red flag behind it. They tell us to sit down and start asking us thousands of questions. One signorina talks while the other writes everything down on a sheet of paper. When we're done, the one who was talking takes a candy out of a tin and hands it to me. The one who was writing takes the sheet and puts it on the desk in front of Mamma. Mamma doesn't know what she's supposed to do. The signorina puts a pen in Mamma's hand and tells her she has to sign. Mamma just sits there. I unwrap the candy and the lemon smell tickles my nose. I don't get to eat candy every day.

From the next room we can hear the three young men shouting. The signorinas look at each other without saying anything, because you can see they're used to it and they know they can't do anything about it. In the meantime, Mamma Antonietta sits there with the sheet in front of her and the pen in her hand, which is hanging by her side. I ask why they're fighting like that in the other room. The one who was writing before says nothing. The other signorina who was talking before says that they're not fighting, they're just deciding what needs to be done, so that everyone can be better off, which she says is what politics is all about. So I say: "Excuse me, don't you all agree up here?" She pulls a face, like when you put an unripe walnut in your mouth and you don't expect it to be bitter, and then she says that even among themselves not everyone agrees with everyone else, there are currents and movements . . . at this point, the one who was writing before gives her a dig with her elbow, as if she's saying too much, and then turns to Mamma and tells her that if she doesn't know how to sign her name, she can put a cross on the dotted line, because they can both be witnesses. Mamma Antonietta blushes bright red and, without lifting her eyes from the paper, draws a slightly crooked X on the page. After everything I'd heard about the currents and movements, I'm feeling a little scared, because Zandragliona always says air currents and movements are what give kids colds and coughs, and I've heard that the sick kids don't get to go on the trains. And that's not fair either, because it's the sick kids who need to go and get taken care of, right? It's easy to talk about solidarity with the healthy kids, as Pachiochia would quite rightly say, since—apart from her mustache and brown gums—she's a nice lady underneath, and every now and again she even gives me two lire coins to spend.

The signorinas write a few more things in a big ledger and then walk with us to the door. When we go through to the other room, the three young men are still arguing about politics. Every two or three exchanges, the thin blond one yells something about "the problem of the south" or "national integration." I watch Mamma closely to see whether she's understood, but she looks straight ahead and keeps on walking. The blond guy turns to me just as I'm passing, as if to say: "You say something. Tell him, will you?" I want to say that it's none of my business and that Mamma Antonietta is the one who brought me here for my own good, otherwise I wouldn't be here, but, before I can open my mouth, Mamma Antonietta yanks my arm and hisses: "You little show-off. Now you want to stick your nose into this stuff, too? Shut your mouth and get out of here!"

So we walk on, the blond guy following us with his eyes until we are out the door.

4

B AD WEATHER HAS COME ALL OF A SUDDEN. Mamma hasn't sent me out looking for rags, partly because it's raining and starting to be cold. She hasn't bought me any other fried pizzas, but she once made me a meat-and-onion *pasta alla genovese* I go crazy for. The nun hasn't showed her face recently, and in the neighborhood they've gotten bored of talking about the train thing.

Since we weren't doing so well at home these days, me and Tommasino went into business together. He wasn't that keen to begin with. Part of him was disgusted and part of him was scared his mother would find out and send him on the train as a punishment. I told him that if Capa 'e Fierro managed to make money with stuff we found in the garbage, we would be stupid not to try. So that is how we started with the sewer rats. Our deal was that I would catch them and he would paint them. We had an upturned box as a stall at the market, in the corner where they sell parrots and goldfinches. Our specialty was hamsters. I had gotten the idea because I'd seen an American officer breeding them and selling them to rich ladies who weren't so rich anymore. They would skin them and make fur collars for their coats, showing off and saving money at the same time. If we cut the tail off the sewer rats I caught and painted them brown and white with shoe polish, they looked just like the American officer's hamsters. Business was going well, and me and Tommasino had built up a good clientele. We would be rich by now if one terrible day it hadn't rained.

"Amerì," Tommasino had said that morning, "if we make enough money, you won't have to go up north with the Communists."

"What does that have to do with anything?" I asked. "It'll be like a vacation."

"A vacation for the chicken shit of this world, you mean. Guess where *we're* going this summer? To the island of Ischia."

At that very moment, the sky went black, and it started pouring with rain like I'd never seen before.

"Tommasino," I said. "The next time you tell a whopper like that, bring an umbrella."

We ran for cover under the cornice of a building, but the stall with the painted sewer rats was still there. Before we even realized, the shoe polish had been washed away, and the hamsters had been transformed back into rats. The ladies around the cages started screaming.

"Ew! They'll give us cholera!"

We couldn't run away because the ladies' husbands were threatening to beat us up. Luckily, Capa 'e Fierro came along. He grabbed both of us by the collar and yelled, "Make that filthy shit go away right now. You and me will be having a good talk later."

I was sure I'd get a good dressing down when I got home, but he didn't mention the sewer rats at all. Then one day, when he came to the door to get down to work with Mamma, he took me aside before going in. He pulled on his cigarette so that all the smoke was inside his mouth and, before letting it out, he said, "It was a good idea. But the stall should have been in the covered market!" He laughed, and the smoke rings grew wider as they rose up into the air. "If you want to go into business, you need to come with me to the market. I'll teach you." He put his hand on my cheek, in what could have been a slap or a caress. It was impossible to tell. Then he left.

I was tempted by the idea of going to Capa 'e Fierro. If only to improve my business skills. But the police came and took him away. I think because of the contraband coffee. People in the neighborhood stopped talking about the painted hamsters, because they were too busy gossiping about Capa 'e Fierro in jail. I'd like to see him saying he'll always be free now!

As soon as Mamma heard the news, she moved all the stuff away but for days, every time she heard a noise behind the door, she hid her face in her hands as if she wanted to disappear underground. Anyway, the police didn't come to our house, and after a few days people had gotten bored of that, too. People always talk up a storm, and then they forget everything. Except Mamma, who hardly ever talks, but remembers everything.

One morning, when I've stopped even thinking about the trains, she wakes me before the sun is out and it is still dark outside the window, puts on her best dress, and combs her hair in front of the mirror. She lays out a set of clothes that are a little less worn-out than usual for me and says: "Let's go, or we'll be late." That's when I get it.

We start walking. Mamma in front; me behind. In the meantime, it has started raining. I play around leaping over the puddles, and Mamma boxes me around the ears, but my feet are already wet, and there's still a long way to go. I look around to see if I can play my shoe game and win some more points, but today I don't feel like it. I'd like to hide my face in my hands, too, and disappear for a bit. There are lots of other mammas with their children walking alongside us. There are some papas too, but you can see they don't want to be there. One of them has written on a sheet of paper a list of instructions: what time his little boy gets up, what time he goes to bed, what he likes and doesn't like to eat, how many times he poops, remember to use a waterproof bed sheet because he wets his bed. He reads the list to his wife, the kid dying of embarrassment in front of all the others, folds it in four, and puts it in the boy's pocket. Then he has second thoughts, takes it out again, and jots down a quick "thank you" to the family that will be taking his son in, saying that, thank God, they are not in need, they would just like their kid to have a nice little vacation.

The ladies stride ahead defiantly, each with two, three, or four children tagging along behind. I'm an only child, since I didn't make it in time to meet my big brother, Luigi. I didn't make it in time to meet my father, either. I was born too late for everyone. It's better this way, though, because this way my father doesn't need to feel ashamed about putting me on the train.

We get to a long, long building. Mamma Antonietta calls it the Reclusorio. She says it's a hospice for the poor. "What?" I say. "Weren't they taking us up north so we could eat and drink? Now we're at the hospice for the poor. Things are getting worse instead of better! Wouldn't it be better if we just stayed home, on our street?" Mamma Antonietta says we're here because, before they can take us north, they need to check us out to see whether we're healthy or sick, whether we're contagious . . .

"And then," Mamma Antonietta says, "they have to give us some warm clothes, coats, and shoes, because up north it's not like down here. They have real winters up there!"

"Brand-new shoes?" I ask.

"Brand-new, or used but new," she says.

"Two points!" I yell.

Forgetting for a moment that I'm about to leave, I start jumping around and around until Mamma grabs me by the arm.

There's a crowd forming in front of the long building. There are mothers with children of all ages: tiny, small, middle-sized, and big. I'm middle-sized. Standing in front of the gate, there's a signorina, but it's not Maddalena. It's not even one of the rice dames. She tells us we need to stand in line, as they're going to check us out and then, she says, they're going to stitch a number on us, so they know who we are. If not, I reckon, when we come back, they'll end up giving every mamma the wrong child. Mamma is the only thing I have, and I don't want to be mistaken for another child, so I cling to her bag and tell her I really don't need new shoes in the end and, if it's for my own good, we can go home immediately. I feel sad in my tummy and I think that if I had carried on dribbling and stuttering, I wouldn't have had to leave.

I turn around, because I don't want her to see me crying, but then I almost burst out laughing. Two rows behind me there's Tommasino.

"Hey, Tommasì," I call out. "Are you waiting for the ferry to Ischia?"

He glares at me, his face as white as a sheet. He's scared stiff, I can see it. In the end, even his mother had to ask for charity!

Pachiochia told me Donna Armida was once rich, very rich. She lived in a fancy building on the Corso and had servants. She used to make clothes for the finest ladies in the city and knew all the people that counted. Her husband, Don Gioacchino Saporito, was nearly, nearly going to buy a car.

Zandragliona, on the other hand, said Donna Armida had gotten ahead, no disrespect, by licking the feet of the Fascists. Then, when fascism went away, she went back to being a rag trader, which was in her nature, and her husband, who had been a big shot under fascism, was arrested and interrogated. Everybody expected some kind of example to be made of him. I don't know, something like a punishment, a conviction, prison. But nobody did anything. Zandragliona said there'd been an armistice, which is like, for example, when Mamma found out I'd broken the casserole dish we used for macaroni which her mamma, Filomena, bless her soul, had left her, she said: "Get out of my sight or I'll beat the living daylights out of you." And I ran away and stayed at Zandragliona's, and didn't show my face back home for two days. Donna Armida's Fascist husband was released and went home, and nothing was ever said again. Now the two of them run their rag trade from a ground-floor tenement apartment in the alley right next to ours.

Tommasino, Donna Armida's little boy, had brand-new shoes (a star-studded prize!) when his mamma was a seamstress. Then, when she went back to being a rag trader and moved to our neighborhood, he still had the same shoes as before, but by that time they were old and full of holes (one point).

When she sees Tommasino, Mamma squeezes my hand to remind me of my promise. I squeeze hers back and turn to Tommasino, winking at him. Sometimes, Tommasino would come to look for rags with me. Donna Armida was not happy because she said her son should be keeping company with his betters, not with people like me who are worse off than him. When Mamma found out, she made me promise not to be friends with Tommasino, because he was the son of ignorant peasants who had made money and then lost it again, and anyhow, they were Fascists, as Zandragliona had said. I promised Mamma and Tommasino promised his. So every afternoon we would meet, but in secret.

More and more children are pouring in, some on foot and others jumping off the free buses that a lady next to us says the bus company has brought in specially. There are even some kids arriving in police jeeps. The jeeps with no soldiers in them, and all those kids carrying colored banners and waving to us, look like carnival floats in the Piedigrotta Festival. I ask Mamma if I can join them in the jeeps. She grips my hand even tighter and tells me to stick right by her side or I'll get lost. And if I really want to get lost, I should wait until they stitch a number on me. The crowd is getting thicker. The signorina tries to get us in line but the line moves all the time, like an eel in the fishmonger's hand.

A little blond girl, who until today has been badgering her mother because she wanted to go on the train trip, is now crying her eyes out, saying she doesn't want to go anymore. A boy, just a little older than me, in a brown hat, who came to see his brother off, is saying it's not fair that he has to stay here when his brother is leaving for the good life, and he starts blubbering, too. There is scolding and tongue-lashing all around but the kids go on wailing, and the mammas don't know which way to turn. In the end, one of the signorinas arrives with the lists and solves the problem. She crosses out the little blond girl's name and puts the name of the boy in the brown hat down instead, making everyone happy. Except the little blond girl's mamma, who storms off saying: "We'll settle this when we get home."

At one point, I hear a voice I know well. Striding in front of the group of ladies marching in a procession is Pachiochia. She's swinging her arms and barking out commands with all the breath in her body. There's a picture of King Umberto I pinned to her breast. The first time I had seen the photo I had said: "Who's this handsome man with the mustache? Your fiancé?" Pachiochia had started kicking me, because I'd offended her dearly departed husband-to-be who'd died in the First World War and whom she'd never betrayed, even in her thoughts, God bless us! Then she'd crossed herself three times, the third time kissing the tips of her fingers and lobbing the kiss up to the sky. Pachiochia had said the handsome man with the mustache was our last king, Umberto, who was finished before he even started, because those people had gotten it into their heads to make our country a republic and cheated with the ballot sheets, so they would win. Pachiochia had said that she was a *mon-ar-chist*, and that the Communists had turned the world upside down and now nothing made any sense at all. Crooks and thugs, the whole lot of them. In fact, she'd said, my father was probably a red Commie crook and a thug himself, and that's why he'd had to get away. America, ha-ha! I thought she could be right, because I have red hair and Mamma's hair is black . . . so the carrot must be from my father. Since then, I don't get upset when people call me "evil hair," as they often do.

Pachiochia, with the portrait on her breast, leads the procession of ladies, who have no kids with them. These women start giving a piece of their mind to the mothers in the crowd with their kids.

"Don't sell your children," they shout. "They've turned your heads with their talk, but the truth is they'll be taking your children to Siberia to put them to work, if they don't die of cold first."

The little ones don't want to leave, and the older ones dig their heels in and say they want to leave. It's like St. Gennaro's feast day, but without the miracles. The more Pachiochia beats her breast, the more she pummels the mustached king who is pinned there. If Zandragliona were here, she would say something back, but she hasn't arrived yet. Pachiochia goes on. "Don't let your children leave! They won't allow them back. Hold your children close, like when we were under the bombs, and you were all they needed to protect them. With Providence on your side."

I remember the wailing of the sirens and everyone screaming. When the bombs came, Mamma would pick me up and run to the shelter with me in her arms. Once we were inside, she would hold me tight all the time. I was happy during the air raids.

The procession of ladies with no children plows past the crowd of mothers and us kids, who have somehow finally managed to get in line, and everything turns into a mess again. A few more signorinas rush out the front door of the long, long building to try to make peace.

"Don't leave," they tell the mothers. "Don't deprive your children of this chance. Think of the winter that's coming. Think of the cold, the trachoma infections, your damp houses . . ."

In the meantime, the signorinas go up to every kid and hand out a little package wrapped in silver foil.

"We're mothers, too," they go on. "Your children will be warm over the winter; they'll have food and they'll be taken care of. There are families in Bologna, Modena, and Rimini waiting to welcome them into their families. They'll come back prettier, healthier, chubbier. They'll have food on their plates every day: breakfast, lunch, and dinner."

Then a signorina comes and gives me a package wrapped in silver foil, too. I tear the wrapper off, and there's a dark brown bar inside.

"Eat it, my sweet boy. It's chocolate!" she says.

"Yeah, I've heard about it," I say, trying to look indifferent.

"Donna Antonietta, are you selling your son, too?" Pachiochia calls out at that very moment, her hand resting on the photo of the mustached king, pounded so much that it is crumpled and almost unrecognizable. "I didn't think you would stoop so low! You are not that needy. Is it because they took Capa 'e Fierro away? If you had asked me, I would have offered you a nice cup of coffee."

Mamma Antonietta gives me an ugly look, convinced I was the coffee spy, but I go on munching my chocolate bar and pretend to keep my eyes closed.

"Donna Pachiochia, I've never asked anything of anyone, and if I ever have, I've always paid everything back. When I can't pay someone back, I don't ask. My husband had to go away to seek his fortune, and when he comes back . . . You know my story. I don't need to explain anything to you."

"What fortune, Donna Antoniè? Who are you kidding? There's no longer any *dig-ni-ty*!"

When Pachiochia says the word *dignity*, I really do close my eyes, so I don't have to see the flecks of spit flying through the gaps in her brown gums. But I open them again when I realize Mamma Antonietta isn't answering, which is never a good sign. Not saying anything when she's being taunted is not like her. So I take the last piece of chocolate out of the foil, crush the silver paper into a little ball, and put it in my pocket so I can use it as a cannonball for a tin soldier I found the day before yesterday on the Corso. In the end, I'm the one that speaks up for Mamma.

"Donna Pachiò, I have a father some place or other. What about you, though? Do you have a child?"

Pachiochia places her hand on her breast and strokes the poor crumpled mustached king.

"You don't, right? Is a portrait of King Umberto all you have left?"

Pachiochia's brown gums quiver with anger.

"What a pity! If you had a child, I'd give him this last piece of chocolate. See this?"

And I toss the whole thing in my mouth.

5

"LADIES, LADIES! LISTEN UP! I'M MADDALENA Criscuolo from Santa Lucia. I fought in the four-day uprising here."

The mothers go quiet. Maddalena stands on a vegetable cart and speaks through a metal funnel that makes her voice louder.

"When we had to drive out the Germans, we women did our part. Mothers, daughters, wives, young and old: we went down into the streets and we fought with our men. You were there, and so was I. This is another battle, but the enemy is more dangerous: hunger and poverty. If you fight now, your children will be the ones to gain something!"

Every mamma looks down at her children.

"They'll come back fatter and more beautiful, and you will be able to rest after the endless toil that life has been for you until today. When you embrace your children again, you, too, will be fatter and more beautiful. I'll bring them back myself; I swear on my honor this is as true as the fact that my name is Maddalena Criscuolo."

Everyone was quiet, even the kids.

Maddalena climbs down from the vegetable cart and starts walking through the crowd of mothers, with kids hanging on to their skirts, and she starts singing through the metal funnel. She has a nice voice, like the ones I hear when I go and sit outside the Conservatory, waiting for Carolina to come out with her violin.

"*Sebben che siamo donne, paura non abbiamo . . .*" she starts. It's a song about a union, where women aren't scared because they are together and they love their children and they want something called socialism: "*Per amor dei nostri figli, socialismo noi vogliamo.*"

The other signorinas follow Maddalena's lead. The mothers stand there in silence, but then a few of them take courage and start singing, too. Then they all join in. That is when Pachiochia and the ladies in her procession start singing the royal anthem: "*Viva il Re!*" Long live the King. The happy trumpets blast. "*Viva il Re! Viva il Re!*" But there are not very many of them, and in any case, they sing out of tune, and so our mammas' voices drown them out as they sing louder and louder and in the end, you can only hear their voices, their kids singing along too. It's the first time I've ever heard Mamma Antonietta sing. Pachiochia clamps her mouth shut, hiding her gums. Then she turns around, positions herself at the head of the procession, and leads her ladies away. As she passes right next to me, I hear her say, "Hunger is stronger than fear . . ." but then the crowd closes around her, and I can't hear the rest.

Maddalena speaks through the metal funnel again and tells us we should say goodbye to our mammas and go into the long, long building because they need to wash us and give us a checkup from a doctor. She promises that the kids who behave will get more chocolate. I hold Mamma's hand tightly, and when I look at her, I see that her eyes are a strange color, like the uniforms of the German soldiers when they came to raid our neighborhood for food. So I open up my arms like I once saw an orchestra conductor doing, when I snuck into the theater with Carolina during a rehearsal for a concert, and I hug Mamma with all my strength. My face is flattened against her belly, and I feel as though my eyes are turning the same color as the German soldiers' uniforms when Pachiochia and Zandragliona made them eat pigeon poop. Mamma Antonietta is surprised, because hugs are not our strong point. But then I feel her hands in my hair moving slowly back and forth. Her hands are soft, like soapstone underwater. It doesn't last long.

One of the signorinas comes up to me and asks my name.

"Amerigo Speranza, like Mamma Antonietta," I answer.

She sticks a card on my shirt with a pin. There's my name, last name, and a number on it. She gives another card just like mine to Mamma, who tucks it into her bra, where she keeps all the important stuff: a little money, a holy card of St. Anthony—the enemy of the devil—a hankie embroidered by her mamma, Filomena—bless her soul—and now this card with my number on it. That way, when I'm gone, she can keep everything close to her heart.

When all the kids and mothers have been given their numbers, Maddalena picks up the metal funnel again and starts talking, her head turning one way then the other so that everyone can hear.

"Ladies, ladies! Don't go away yet. Wait a moment. Stand in a line everyone, each mother with her children in front of her, so we can take a photograph."

The mothers are so stunned by this idea that they all start milling around again, breaking up the line that took God Almighty himself to form. One of them straightens her hair, another pinches her cheeks to make them rosy, yet another bites her lips to make them look like she's got lipstick on: she's seen it in the portraits of the ladies in the photographer's window on the Corso. Mamma Antonietta licks her hand and wets my hair, which is growing fast after my melon crew cut, to make a parting. Maddalena walks through the crowd and divides the mothers and children into groups. She's holding a big piece of card with writing on it.

"What does it say, Amerì?" my mother asks. I look at the letters. I can read some of them, but not all of them. I get muddled up when I try and put them together. I like numbers better.

"What did I send you to school for? To warm up the chair?"

Luckily, Maddalena picks up the funnel and reads it out to all of us. It says that we're the children of the south whom northern Italians are waiting to host, and that this is called solidarity. I wanted to ask her what *solidarity* meant, but a big boy in a jacket and slightly worn-out gray pants tells us to get ready for the photograph. When everyone is in position, Mamma Antonietta puts a hand on my shoulder. I turn around to look at her. It almost looks as though she's smiling, but at the last minute, she changes her mind and pulls her same old face.

Finally, we get to go inside the long, long building. We all look smaller without our mammas next to us, even the boys who were acting tough while we were waiting outside. The signorinas put us into rows of three and leave us in the dark corridor.

I GO AND STAND RIGHT NEXT TO TOMMASINO, whose legs are shaking worse than the drenched hamsters when they were turning back into sewer rats. I wanted to give him some courage. The third kid in our row is a thin little girl with short hair called Mariuccia. She's the cobbler's little girl, the one who resoles shoes up on Pizzofalcone. I recognize her, because Mamma Antonietta had once taken me to her father to ask whether he could teach me the trade, since I was so obsessed with shoes. The shoe mender had looked at me, then at my mother, and finally he had pointed behind the counter: there were four kids of different ages with shoes, nails, and glue in their hands. They were the four kids his wife, bless her soul, had had the courage to burden him with before disappearing to the other world. Mariuccia was the only girl, and one day, when she was a little older, she would keep house and look after her brothers. Anyway, at that time, the father was keeping all four kids in the shop as apprentice shoe-menders, so his answer to Mamma had been no.

Zandragliona had told me that when Maddalena and the others went and talked to him about the trains, the cobbler decided to send Mariuccia, since the others were boys and could be useful in the shop. Mariuccia was a girl, but she didn't even know how to heat up leftover macaroni, so she wasn't good for anything. When we were told to get into a line, Mariuccia's face was white and her eyes wild. "I don't want to go. I don't want to! They'll cut off my hands and put me in the oven!"

There were other kids who were so desperate to leave, they were calling out: "I have an eye infection," "I have trachoma," as if they had hit the jackpot rather than caught a disease. And then all the others started acting important and yelling, "We have trachoma, we have trachoma," because they thought that they would only let you get on the train if you had trachoma.

Me, Mariuccia, and Tommasino sit next to one another. Every

now and again, Mariuccia sniffs the air. But she can't smell any burning or cooked flesh and she can't see any smoke. So, for now, they're not putting us in a gas oven. All we see are signorinas running up and down and stopping in front of a tall young man holding a big ledger, where every now and again he jots something down with a pencil. They call him Comrade Maurizio. He walks up and down, too. He listens to everyone and has an answer to every question. When he comes up to us, he stops and looks at us.

"And you? What are your names?"

We're too embarrassed to answer.

"Hey, I'm talking to you. Don't you have any tongues?" he asks, laughing. "Did they cut them off or something?"

"Well, not yet," Tommasino says, scared to death.

"Why? Are they going to cut them off?" Mariuccia asks. "So, Pachiochia was right after all."

Comrade Maurizio laughs again. Then he gives us each a pat on the head.

"Come on, show me. Stick them out!"

We all three look at one another and then stick our tongues out.

"If it were up to me, I'd cut the tips off because they're a bit too long for my taste . . ."

Mariuccia pulls her tongue back in and crosses her hands in an X over her mouth.

". . . but the regulations don't allow it . . ."

Comrade Maurizio flicks through the pages of the ledger he's holding.

". . . you see, it's written here. Can you read? No? What a pity. If you could, I would show you. It says here in the regulations of the Committee for Children's Salvation, Article 103: It is forbidden to cut children's tongues off . . ." and off he goes, laughing again.

Then he turns the book around and shows us a blank page.

"Comrade Maurizio likes joking!" Tommasino says, some color coming back to his cheeks.

"Bravo! That's exactly right!" Comrade Maurizio says. "And there's something else I like doing too. Sit still for five minutes."

He starts drawing with his pencil on the blank page he showed us. He looks at us and then draws, stops, looks at us again, and draws a little more. He looks at the page, looks back at us, and then rips the page out of the ledger. Our faces are on the sheet of paper. Spitting images. He gives the sheet to Tommasino, who puts it in his pocket.

From the end of the corridor, two signorinas in white coats and white gloves tell us to take our clothes and shoes off. Tommasino, Mariuccia, and I look at one another and start crying. Tommasino because he's scared they'll take away his old shoes full of holes, Mariuccia because she's embarrassed to strip naked in front of everyone, and me because my underpants are patched up and my socks are dirty. So I go up to one of the signorinas in a white coat and gloves and I tell her I can't take my clothes off, because I'm cold, and my two friends follow my example.

Luckily, Maddalena comes along.

"Let's play a new game, okay?" she says. "A game you've never played before!"

Tommasino stops blubbering and stares at her.

"But if we're going to play this game, you need to take your clothes off. Then we'll give you some new clothes that are nice and warm."

"Shoes, too?" I chip in.

"New shoes for everyone!" she says, tucking her hair behind her ears.

The three of us strip off, and Maddalena takes us into another room with some pipes that spray water from the ceiling. It's kind of like rain, but it's hot.

I stand under the pipe and feel the first drops falling. I keep my eyes tightly shut as I'm scared of drowning, but then Maddalena comes up to me with a sponge and soap and covers me with sweet-smelling bubbles. She washes my hair, my arms, my legs, my feet. The soapy aroma reminds me of Carolina, who smelled of violets when we hid in the theater listening to music, and I get a tickly feeling in my belly. When I open my eyes, I see Tommasino next to me splashing, and Mariuccia stamping her feet in a gray puddle.

Maddalena lathers and rinses the other two and then she wraps us all in rough white sheets. After our shower, she takes us into another room where all the kids who have already been washed are sitting on wooden benches, every one of them wrapped in a rough white sheet. Then a Communist signorina does the rounds with a basket full of bread rolls on her arm, and hands us one roll each. She tells us the bread is from the doctor who is going to be giving us a checkup; the one in the room next door. I've never seen a doctor before, and I don't want to start now. In the meantime, though, I eat my bread with my eyes shut, breathing in the strong smell of soap.

6

THE TRACKS AT THE PIAZZA GARIBALDI RAIL-
way station are full of rubble, and the trains have been
damaged by the bombing. A bit like the soldiers I once saw at a
parade, who were waving flags, but who were all incomplete: some
missing an arm, others a leg, others again an eye. The wrecked
train cars looked like war veterans. They are wounded trains, but
they are not dead.

The ones still working, though, are gigantic. You can see the
head of the train but not the tail. Maddalena told us that our
mammas would be coming to say goodbye when we leave, but
I'm pretty sure they won't recognize us when they see us. Luckily,
we still have our numbers pinned onto our coats, otherwise they
would mistake us for northern kids and they wouldn't even be
able to bless our journey with a little prayer, like "May the Virgin
Mary be with you."

Tommasino and all the other boys have had their hair cut,

and they are dressed in shorts and thick socks, a woolen undershirt, a shirt, and a coat. They left my hair as it was, because my head had already been shorn to look like a melon. The girls have all had their hair braided and tied up with red and green ribbons, and they are wearing little dresses or skirts, with coats on top, too. Then there are the shoes. Every child has a new pair of shoes. I've counted so many star-studded prizes that I've won the championship. Only, when it was my turn, Maddalena told me they'd run out of my size. So they gave me a brand-new, shiny pair of brown shoes with laces. But they were one size too small.

"How do they fit? Are you comfortable?"

I tried walking in them, taking a few steps back and forth, and they were too tight. But I was so scared they would take them away again that I said, "Fine. Fine. They're fine," and so I kept them.

They lined us up in front of the train and they gave us instructions: don't dirty anything, don't shout, don't open the windows, don't exchange shoes or pants, don't untie your braids. Then, since we were hungry again, after the bread rolls, they gave us two slices of cheese. But there was no more chocolate.

When I saw the train, I boasted a little and said that my father had taken a train when he went to America; if he had waited for me to be born, we could have set off together. Mariuccia said, "You can't go to America on a train; you need a ship." I said, "What do you know about America? Your father has never even been there," and she said, "You moron, everyone knows that America is on the other side of the sea." Mariuccia is older than me, and she says she went to school for a while before her mother had had the bad idea to die and leave her and her brothers alone with their cobbler father. If Zandragliona were here, I could ask her if America really was on the other side of the sea and whether it's true you can only get there by ship. But Zandragliona's not here and neither is Mamma Antonietta. Not that she would know, because knowing things is not her strong point. The person who is here is the blond Communist with the sad face. The one who was arguing with his comrades in the apartment in Via Medina. He helps Maddalena count the kids, and when he's with her, he doesn't look so sad after all. Maybe she managed to solve that "problem of the south" for him; the one that was making him so worked up and unhappy.

From far away, the train is the spitting image of a model train I once saw in a toy-store window on the Corso. As it comes closer, it gets bigger and bigger and then it's suddenly ginormous. Tommasino hides behind me, he's so scared. He doesn't realize how scared I am, too.

The signorinas check the numbers pinned onto our coats, and read our names from a list. "Amerigo Speranza," one of the signorinas calls out when it's my turn. I climb up three iron steps and find myself inside the train. It's damp and smells soggy, like Pachiochia's ground-floor apartment. From the outside it looks big, but inside it's narrow and cramped, with a long line of compartments, one after the other, each one with a door that you open and close with an iron handle. Now that I'm here, it feels like everything has gone so fast that, even if I wanted to, I wouldn't be able to go back. Mamma must be home now in our tenement apartment, and I feel sad in my stomach. Mariuccia and Tommasino climb up after me. We look at one another, and I can see they're unsure, too, as if they're thinking, "What the heck are we doing here?" The signorinas go on calling names, and the train slowly fills up with kids. Some are sitting, others are standing, still others are running from one compartment to another; some are hungry, some are thirsty, and some others are crying. Comrade Maurizio appears, the one who wanted to cut our tongues off but then drew a picture of us, and walks from one compartment to the next saying, "Quiet, quiet now. Sit down, everybody. It's a long journey." But we keep misbehaving. He's not laughing now. I think that he must be fed up, too, and that soon they're going to take everything away from us. The train, the shoes, the coats. We don't deserve them, Pachiochia's right. We don't deserve anything. I sit on the wooden train bench, rest my face against the stained wall of the compartment, and feel my eyes pricking with tears, because of the soggy smell, the wooden seat, the dirty wall, and because I'm thinking about Mamma.

Then I hear Tommasino and Mariuccia shouting: "Amerigo, Amerì! Get over here! Run! Look out there!"

I get up and race to the window. I push my way past the heads of all the other kids who are all reaching out of the carriage window, straining to touch their mothers' hands. Tommasino moves over a little so that I can see Mamma Antonietta. She looks smaller, in the middle of all the other mothers. It feels like she's far away, even though the train hasn't moved yet. Zandragliona is standing next to her. She's come to say goodbye to me, even though she had a memorial service for a relative today. Mamma comes right up to the window and puts something in my hand. It's a small, red, round apple. An annurca apple. I stick it in my pocket to keep it safe. I think it's so beautiful, I'll never eat it. It looks to me like a red heart, like the one I once saw when

I crept in and hid in the Sansevero Chapel. Zandragliona had told me there were two live skeletons, complete with bones, and veins, and hearts, and everything. So I ventured into the dark chapel. When I lit a candle, I saw two bright white statues that seemed to be walking out of the stone they were carved in. The closer I got with the candle, the more alive they looked. There was also a Jesus Christ made of marble, lying under a sheet that was also made of stone. It looked like he was breathing in his sleep, and as if the sheet covering him were so light that he might wake up at any moment. I started walking between the statues, my heart beating in my head, and that's when I saw them. The two skeletons were standing there, alive as anything, as if they'd been flesh and bone a minute before. Their heads were shiny, with no hair. They were smiling, with no teeth. Their bones were tied together in a tangle of red and blue veins. In the middle was a red heart, as round and red as an annurca apple. I dropped the candle and found myself in the dark again. I groped around but I couldn't find the way out, so I started screaming, but nobody came. I somehow managed to get to the door, and, once I was outside, I saw that night had fallen. But the dark was nothing compared to the blackness in the chapel. I still have nightmares about Prince Sangro's skeletons, every now and again.

I look at Mamma through the window. She's wrapped up in her shawl in silence. Silence is her strong point. Then the train suddenly screeches, louder than my teacher with the pointed chin when she found the dead beetle we had hidden in her alphabet book. All the mothers on the platform start waving their arms frantically. It looks like they're saying goodbye, but they're not.

All the kids on the train shrug themselves out of their coats and start pushing them through the open windows into their mothers' arms. Mariuccia and Tommasino take theirs off, too.

"For the love of God, what are you doing?" I ask them. "Up in northern Italy you'll be dying of cold."

"We promised," Tommasino explained. "The kids who get to go on the train have to leave their coats to the brothers and sisters who are left behind, because the winter is cold up in northern Italy, but it's not warm here, either."

"What about us?"

"The Communists will give us another coat, because they're rich and they can afford it," Mariuccia explains, as she throws her coat to her cobbler father, who puts it straight onto one of her motherless brothers.

I don't know what to do: I don't have any siblings. My big brother, Luigi, could have done with it a while back, but he has no use for it now. Then I think that Mamma could always turn it around and make a jacket for herself out of my coat. So I slip it off and throw it to her. I'm keeping the apple, though. Mamma Antonietta catches it in midair and looks at me. It's almost as if she's smiling.

The signorinas start shouting from the compartments on both sides. I stay at the window to see what is going on. The station-master walks up and down the platform not knowing what to do: whether to stop the train to get the coats back, or order us all off as a punishment for double-crossing them . . . Comrade Maurizio leaps off the train in a hurry to talk to the stationmaster. The stationmaster says they'll hitch a radiator car to our train to make it warmer.

So, with the signorinas scolding us, the mothers stampeding to get away with our coats tucked under their arms, and the children on the train laughing, the stationmaster waves his flag and the train lurches forward. It starts slowly, slowly, and then gains a little speed. Mamma Antonietta is in a corner of the station that is getting farther and farther away. She's holding my coat to her breast. As if she were holding me tight during the air raids.

7

N OW THAT THEY'VE TAKEN OUR COATS, HOW are they going to recognize us?" Mariuccia asks, worried sick.

"Well, by our faces, right?" Tommasino answers.

"Okay, but how will the Communists know who I am and who you are? We all look the same to them, like black American soldiers do to us. We're all kids who are dying of hunger. There's no difference between us. How are they going to give us back the right mamma at the end?"

"I think they did it on purpose," a kid with yellow hair and a gap three teeth wide in his mouth says. "They must have told our mothers to take our coats, so that when we get to Russia, they can't find us."

"And we'll die of cold," another kid next to him adds.

Mariuccia looks at me, her eyes welling, to see whether this is true.

"Did you know that in Russia they eat babies for breakfast?" the boy with gaps in his mouth says to Mariuccia, who is as white as a sheet.

"Well, they'll be sending *you* back, then, since you're all skin and bones . . ." I say. "And anyway, who told you we were going to Russia? I heard we were going up to northern Italy."

Mariuccia looks a little calmer but the boy with the straw-colored hair goes on.

"They only say northern Italy to convince our mothers. But the truth is they're taking us to Russia and they'll put us in houses made of ice, with ice beds, ice tables, and ice sofas . . ."

Mariuccia starts crying silently. Tommasino holds her hand tight while her tears fall onto her new dress.

"Sure. We'll have a nice *granita* then. What flavor do you like your water ice, Mariù? Lemon or coffee?"

Comrade Maurizio comes into our compartment with a tall, thin man wearing glasses. The kids start teasing him: four-eyes, goggles, blinkers, you name it.

"Be quiet, the lot of you!" Comrade Maurizio shouts. "You may not know it, but if you're on this train it's all thanks to this person here."

"Who is this person, then?" the short dark boy asks.

"My name is Gaetano Macchiaroli," the man in the glasses says, in good Italian, not dialect. "My main job is making books."

We are so quiet that anyone would think our tongues had actually been cut out.

"I organized this nice trip for you, together with other comrades."

"Why? What do you get out of it? You're not our father or our mother," the short, dark-faced boy challenges. He's the only one that isn't scared.

"When necessary, we are all fathers and mothers of those in need. That's why we're taking you to stay with people who will take care of you and treat you as if you were their children, for your own good."

"So, are they going to shave our hair off, so we look like melons?" I ask, almost in a whisper.

The man in glasses doesn't hear me. He waves his hands in the air as if he's saying goodbye.

"Have a great trip, kids! Be good and have fun!"

When the tall, thin man leaves the compartment, nobody dares breathe.

Comrade Maurizio sits down right next to us and opens his ledger.

"Since you all decided to give your mothers your coats with your names and numbers written on them"—and he looks each and every one of us straight in the eye—"now we have to identify you again from scratch. In this ledger there are all the lists of all the children, car by car." He says he wants to know our first name, last name, mother's name, and father's name. We answer one by one, and he pins a card with our name on the sleeve. When he comes to the blond boy with no teeth, Maurizio has to ask him his name two or three times, but he never opens his mouth. He pretends to be deaf and dumb. Maurizio tries calling him different names to see if he will react. Pasquale, Giuseppe, Antonio. Nothing. Maurizio gets fed up and goes to the next compartment.

"Why are you playing deaf and dumb?" Tommasino asks him. "You were driving the poor guy crazy."

The blond boy gives us a nasty smile.

"You'd have to be dumb to tell them your name," he says, making a rude gesture.

"How will they identify you, then?" Mariuccia asks. "Aren't you scared they won't give you back to your mother?"

"My mother?" the blond boy says. "She's the one who told me that anyone working in contraband should never, ever tell anyone their name, or where they live, or who their family are. Even in an air raid. Especially to the police!"

The blond boy makes a face as if to say he's better than us and know things we don't. We're all quiet. Him, too. I'm pretty sure he's getting scared that, after acting so smart, they won't know who to give him back to.

After a while, another signorina I haven't seen before comes in. She sits down with the lists in her hands and starts again. When it's my turn, she asks me my name.

"Amerigo Speranza," I say.

"Age?"

"Seven."

"Father and mother?"

"Antonietta Speranza."

"And what's your father's name? What does he do?"

"I don't know," I say, flushed with embarrassment.

"You don't know what job your father does?" she asks.

"I don't know if I have a father or if I don't. Some say I do; others say I don't. Mamma Antonietta says he left. Pachiochia says he ran away . . ."

"Shall we write 'missing,' then?"

"Can we leave it blank so that when he comes back, we can fill it in?" I ask.

The signorina looks at me, lifts her pen, and moves on to the line below.

"Next!" she says.

8

THE JOURNEY IS LONG. ALL THE SHOUTING, wailing, and laughing when we pulled out of the station has gone. All you can hear is the rolling of the train, hammering the same rhythm all the way. Then there's the stink of warmed-up damp. I sit and stare out the window, like all the others. I think about the spot in Mamma's bed where I sleep, with Capa 'e Fierro's stashes of coffee hidden under it. I think about the streets where I roam all day, rain or shine, looking for rags. I think about Pachiochia, who must by this time be in bed in her tenement apartment with the picture of the mustached king on her bedside table. I think about Zandragliona, and I can almost smell her onion frittata. I think about the alleyways where I live, which are narrower and shorter than this train. I think about my father, who has gone to America, and my big brother, Luigi, who has gone to the other world with his bronchial asthma and left me to leave on the train all on my own.

While I'm thinking, I nod off every now and again. My head

lolls, my eyes close, and my thoughts get all mixed up. Nearly everyone is asleep around me. I look out the window a little longer. I see the moon running over the fields, as if it were playing tag with the train. I pull my legs up onto the bench and put my arms around them. Hot, sticky tears are rolling down my cheeks and running into my mouth. They are salty and they ruin the memory of the flavor of chocolate. Tommasino is fast asleep in front of me. He of all people, who is scared of his own shadow during the day! And look at me. I used to be brave enough to go down into the sewers and catch rats, and now all I want is for the train to stop, and for everyone to come and get me and take me back. All I want is to hear Mamma's voice saying, "Amerì, come along now. It's time to go home!"

Just as I am about to doze off, there is a screech that makes my skin crawl, like nails scratching the bottom of a saucepan. The train comes to an abrupt halt, and we are all thrown off our seats, one on top of the other. I find myself facedown on the floor. Mariuccia, who was fast asleep, starts crying, scared that she had torn her new dress. The lights go out and we are plunged into the dark.

"Who gave this guy his license?" the blond boy calls out from somewhere in the compartment.

"Maybe we're there," Tommasino says.

"No," said another boy, who had gotten on the train with us and told the signorinas his name was Mimmo. "Mamma told me that we have to wait the whole night, and then we arrive tomorrow evening."

"I bet they throw us all out of the train and leave us in the dark," says someone, maybe the blond boy, but maybe another boy, making the most of the dark when we can't see anyone's face, to frighten us to death.

"I think the train has broken down," I say, holding Mariuccia's hand tight, to give her courage, and maybe to give myself some, too. I'm actually thinking that the Fascists have blown up the line to stop us leaving, like Pachiochia said they would. Mariuccia starts blubbering again anyway:

"We're going to die either of cold or of hunger."

I put my hands over my ears, screw up my eyes, and wait for the explosion. But nothing happens. Maybe Maddalena managed to stop them just in time. That's what she won her medal for, after all. For saving the bridge in the Sanità quarter. In the darkness I feel the icy, bony fingers of the Prince of Sangro's skeletons at the back of my neck. So I open my eyes and unblock my ears. We hear the door of the compartment open. Nobody says a word. Nobody breathes. We are completely still.

"Who pulled the alarm?" Maddalena says, just as the lights come back on. Her face is serious, and she's so nervous her forehead is split down the middle with a deep gray line. "Trains are not a joking matter," she says, looking annoyed and staring at the blond boy. He understands and acts offended. I think he's regretting not giving his name, just a little. Because now they're going to blame him for every single thing. It serves him right.

"We didn't pull it!" Tommasino says, getting the toothless smuggler out of trouble, too.

"We were all asleep," Mariuccia adds, now that she has stopped crying, because her dress is still as good as new.

"It doesn't matter who it was," Maddalena says. "Whoever it was, you need to keep your hands to yourselves and not touch anything else, or tomorrow you'll spend the day at the police station."

"Which lever stops the train? Is it the red one?" the blond smart-ass smuggler asks.

"I'm not so stupid that I would tell you!" Maddalena answers.

The boy realizes she's kidding him and shuts up.

"Anyway, I'll stay here now. We'll have one of us in every compartment to keep an eye on you. That way, we can avoid any further unplanned stops!"

Maddalena sits in a corner and smiles. She's never sad. It's like she has a light on inside her eyes at all times. Maybe that's why they gave her a medal.

9

EVERYONE IS ASLEEP EXCEPT ME. I DON'T LIKE the silence. In the street where I live, it's always noon, even at night. Life never stops, even when there's been a war. Instead, here I am looking through the window and all I can see are ruins. Upside-down tanks, wrecked airplane fuselages, bombed buildings only half standing. I feel sadness welling up in my belly. Like that time when Mamma Antonietta sang me a lullaby that goes *"Ninnaò, Ninnaò, questo bimbo a chi lo do . . ."* and it sent all my sleepiness away, because the person in the song is giving the baby to a bogeyman, who's going to keep it for a whole year. But then, even the bogeyman doesn't want the baby anymore, and he gives it to someone else, and that person gives it to someone else again, and then you never know what happens to the baby in the end.

The train stops every now and again and more children get on. The screaming, crying, and laughing starts again, but not for long. Then the quiet comes back, and there's only the chugging of the train and the sad feeling in my belly. When I was sad, back home, I'd usually go to Zandragliona's apartment. Before leaving, I had put all my precious things in an old tin box that Mamma Antonietta had given me, and she had hidden it under a tile where she keeps her precious stuff, too. Pachiochia says Zandragliona keeps all her money under a tile, but I think she's just jealous.

Tommasino turns in his sleep and mutters something I can't make out. He's dreaming. He opens his eyes, laughs, and then goes back to sleep. Maybe he's dreaming of Capajanca's fruit cart, the Commie ovens, his mother's lashings when he came home after the hamster fiasco, who knows? Whatever he's dreaming, lucky him. At least he's asleep! I'd rather have bad dreams than waking nightmares.

Zandragliona says that when sleep doesn't come to you, you shouldn't go looking for it. So I get up from the train seat and go out of the compartment. The corridor is long and narrow. I start walking up and down and, every now and again, I peek into the other compartments. There are so many faces, so many kids piled on top of one another. They've all fallen asleep as if they were home, as if nothing had happened. I think about my mamma. When I go to bed, I put my cold feet between her thighs, and she starts yelling, "What do you take me for? Your personal bed warmer? Get these slabs of stockfish off me!" But then she takes my feet and warms them up with her hands, toe by toe, and I fall asleep with my toes in her fingers.

I walk back along the corridor to our compartment, but I don't open the door. I pull out the folding seat in the corridor and sit with my forehead against the window. It's dark outside. I can't see a thing. Who knows where we are, how far we are from home, and how long it will take to arrive, nobody even knows where. The window is cold and wet, and my face is dripping. It's a good thing, because at least no one will know I am crying. But Maddalena notices. She sits next to me and gives me a pat. Maybe sleep didn't come to her either.

"Why are you crying?" she asks. "Do you miss your mamma?"

I hide my tears, but accept her caresses.

"No, no, not a bit. I'm not crying for my mamma. It's my shoes. They're too tight."

"Why don't you take them off now that it's nighttime? That way you'll be more comfortable. There's still a long way to go."

"Signorina, thank you, but I'm scared someone will steal them, and I will have to wear someone else's shoes again. I don't want to wear other people's shoes ever again."

IO

ALL OF A SUDDEN, THERE IS A DAZZLINGLY bright light after all the darkness. The train has come out of a tunnel, and a big moon lights up the sky. Everything is white: the streets, the trees, the mountains, the houses. There are lots of white bread crumbs falling, some big and some small.

"It's snowing!" I say out loud to convince myself. "It's snowing! It's snowing!" I say again, louder this time. But nobody wakes up. Not even the boy with the straw-colored hair, who said they were taking us to live in ice houses. I'd like to see his face now, him and his Russia! I rest my head against the window again and follow the snowflakes as they flutter down. That is how my eyes finally close.

Mariuccia wakes me up, screaming like crazy.

"There's ricotta cheese everywhere!"

She runs up to me and shakes me.

"Amerigo, Amerì . . . wake up! There's ricotta all over the

ground. On the streets. On the trees. On the mountains! It's raining ricotta . . ."

The night is over, and a pale ray of sunlight shines through the window.

"Mariù, it's not cream or ricotta cheese. It's snow . . ."

"Snow?"

"Frozen water."

"Like the one Don Mimmì sells from his cart?"

"Kind of, but without the black-cherry syrup on top."

My eyes are still sticky with sleep, and they burn when I try to open them. The white snow shines through the window, and I can't see anything else. It's cold in the train. All the kids' faces are glued to the windows, staring at the white outside.

"Have you never seen snow?" Maddalena asks.

Mariuccia shakes her head, a little ashamed for mistaking snow for ricotta cheese.

"*Signorì*," she says. "When we get there, are they going to give us something to eat? I'm dying of hunger, worse than at home . . ."

Maddalena laughs. It's her way of answering questions. First, she laughs; then she speaks. She says Mariuccia is right, and that when we get there, all the comrades of central Italy will be waiting for us. There will be a big party, with a brass band, banners, and lots of things to eat.

"Are they happy we're going there, then?" I ask her.

"Weren't they forced to take us?" Mariuccia adds.

Maddalena says they weren't. They're happy to have us.

"But why are they happy that we are coming to eat all their food?"

"Because it is their way of expressing sol-i-dar-i-ty," Maddalena says.

"You mean like dig-ni-ty?" I ask.

Maddalena says solidarity is like dignity toward other people. She says we need to help one another. "If I have two salami today, I should give one to you, so that if you have two *caciotta* cheeses tomorrow, you can give one to me."

I think this sounds like a good idea. But I also think that if people in northern Italy have two salami today, and they give one to me, how am I supposed to give them a *caciotta* tomorrow when, until yesterday, I didn't even have any shoes?

"I tasted salami once," Tommasino mumbles, still half asleep. "A grocer in Foria gave me a slice . . ."

"Did he really give it to you?" Mariuccia says, digging her elbows into Tommasino's side, signaling with her hand that maybe he stole it.

Tommasino flushes, and I change the subject, because I know him only too well. Maddalena luckily doesn't hear a thing, because all the kids have started shrieking again. I look out the window and see what all the fuss is about. On the other side of the beach, covered in snow, there's the sea. But it's different from the sea I know. It's as still and smooth as a cat's fur.

"What now? You've never seen the sea before?" Maddalena asks.

"I know the sea," Tommasino says.

"Mamma Antonietta says that the sea has no purpose, except to give us cholera and weak lungs."

"Is that true, signorina?" Mariuccia, who never trusts anyone, asks.

"The sea is for swimming in," Maddalena answers. "For diving and having fun."

"Will the Communists up in northern Italy let us dive?" Mariuccia asks.

"Yes, they will!" Maddalena says. "But not now. It's too cold. When it's the right season."

"I can't swim," Tommasino says.

"What?" I tease him. "You were going to have a vacation on Ischia, don't you remember?"

He crosses his arms and turns the other way.

"They're only taking us to the sea so they can drown us," the blond boy says, without actually believing it. He's just trying to stir Mariuccia up.

"They're tongue waggers, that's all," Maddalena says. "You shouldn't take any notice."

"Excuse me, do you have any children?" Mariuccia asks, doubtful as ever.

Maddalena, for the first time since I met her, makes a sad face.

"Why would she have kids?" I say, to get on Maddalena's good side. "She's far too young!"

"But if you had kids, would you put them on the train or not?" the blond boy asks.

"You don't get it!" I cut in. "Only the needy kids get to go on the train, not the ones who are doing okay. Otherwise, it wouldn't be solidarity, would it?"

Maddalena nods, but doesn't say anything.

"Tell me something, signorina," Mariuccia says with a mischievous grin. "That blond man at the station who was helping you count us kids. . . . Is he your sweetheart?"

"What sweetheart? Sweetheart indeed!" I say, since Maddalena is not speaking anymore. "He's a Communist, too. I saw him at the Party headquarters before leaving."

"So what? What does that mean?" Mariuccia insists. "Just

because you're a Communist doesn't mean you can't be a sweet-heart, right?"

"That Communist?" I answer. "He has the 'problem of the south' to deal with; he's not going to be thinking about love."

"Love has many different faces," Maddalena says. "Not just the ones you're thinking about. For example, isn't being here, with all you disobedient pests, love? And your mothers, who let you come on the train to go far away to Bologna and Rimini and Modena... isn't that love, too?"

"Why? Does somebody who sends you away love you, then?"

"Amerigo, sometimes letting you go shows greater love than keeping you."

I don't understand but I don't answer back, either. Maddalena says she has to go check on the kids in the other compartments to make sure everyone is okay, and so she leaves. Me, Tomma-sino, and Mariuccia start playing rock, paper, scissors to pass the time. After a while, the train slows down and finally stops. The signorinas tell us to hold hands and form a line, two by two; to be good, and to wait quietly until it is our turn to go out. Once we are out in the street, we need to stay put, otherwise we will get lost, and then where would the solidarity go if we were all in different places?

When we pull into the station, there's a band playing, and a white banner that one of the signorinas reads us. It says, "Welcome to the children from the Mezzogiorno." They have come all the way here to welcome us. It's like the festival of Our Lady of the Arch, except there are no people dressed in white, throwing them-selves on the ground in convulsions, shouting *"Madonna dell'Arco"* because they've received a miracle.

The musicians are playing a song all the signorinas know, because they keep shouting *"bella ciao ciao ciao"* and, when the song finishes, they hold their fists up to the sky. The sky is gray and full of long, thin clouds. Mariuccia and Tommasino think they are making fists because they are fighting, but I know it is the Communist salute, because Zandragliona has taught me. It's different from the Fascist salute, which I know, because Pachiochia has taught me. In fact, when crossing paths in our alleyway, Zandragliona and Pachiochia greeted each other with their own salutes, and it looked just like they were playing rock, paper, scissors.

I hold hands with Mariuccia in one row and Tommasino is behind, holding a slightly bigger girl's hand. We walk through the crowd of people waving white, red, and green flags and smiling, clapping, and shouting hello. It feels like we have won a prize, and we have come to northern Italy as a favor to them, not vice versa. Some men in hats with thick mustaches wave red flags with a yellow half-circle in the middle, singing a song I don't know. Every now and again I hear the word *in-ter-na-zio-nale*.

After a while, the ladies start singing, too. They are the wives of the men in hats with thick mustaches carrying the red flags with the yellow half-circle in the middle. I know the song they are singing, because it's the one Maddalena sang through the metal funnel to send Pachiochia away. The one about the women who are not afraid, even if they are women. Or maybe because they are women; I'm not sure. Their voices are getting louder, and many of them look like they are crying as they are singing. I can't understand all the words, because they must be in the language of the north, but I know it's about mothers and children, for one thing, because the signorinas from the train and the Communist ladies from northern Italy look at us and smile as if we were all their own children.

We are led into the big room full of Italian flags and red flags. There's a long, long table in the middle full of good things to eat: cheese, ham, salami, bread, pasta . . . Us kids were desperate to throw ourselves on the food, but a signorina shouts into the metal funnel.

"Children, there's enough for everyone. Don't move. You will each get a plate, a napkin, tableware, and a glass of water. As long as you are here, you will never suffer hunger."

The kids look around wide-eyed and dig one another in the ribs as if to say, "Today's our lucky day; what was that about Communists eating babies?"

Gradually, we get closer to the food, and you could hear a pin drop. Mariuccia, Tommasino, and I sit next to one another. On our plates, there's a slice of pink ham full of white spots, one soft cheese, one as hard as a rock, and one that stinks of smelly feet. We look at one another, but none of us starts eating, even though we are starving. You can read it in our eyes. Luckily, Maddalena soon arrives.

"What's up now? Aren't you hungry any longer?"

"Signorina . . ." Mariuccia says, "are you sure these northerners haven't given us their old food? The ham is full of white spots and the cheese is soft and moldy."

"Of course, they want to poison us," the blond boy with no teeth says.

"If I wanted to get cholera, I'd prefer to eat the mussels down at the port, with all due respect," Tommasino says.

Maddalena picks up a slice of the ham with white spots on it and puts it in her mouth. She says we have to get used to these new specialties: Bologna ham, Parmesan, and Gorgonzola . . .

I pluck up courage and try a little piece of the ham with spots on it. Mariuccia and Tommasino gape at me. They can see from my face, though, that it's delicious, and so they tuck in, too. And then there is no stopping us. We polish off everything, including the soft cheese, the one with the green mold in it, and even the rock-hard, salty one that prickles your taste buds.

"Don't they have mozzarella cheese here?" Tommasino asks.

"You can eat mozzarella back home in Mondragone," Maddalena jokes.

Then a Communist signorina comes around with a trolley full of little cups with white foam inside.

"It's ricotta, it's ricotta," Mariuccia says.

"It's snow, it's snow," Tommasino says.

I pick up a teaspoon and stick a blob of white foam into my mouth: it's freezing and it tastes of milk and sugar. It's soft, iced milk.

"It's ricotta with sugar!" Mariuccia insists.

"It's grated ice with milk!" Tommasino answers.

Mariuccia eats it slowly, leaving a tiny bit in the cup.

"What's wrong? Don't you like ice cream?" Maddalena asks.

"Not really," Mariuccia says, but we all know it's a fib.

"Well, if you really don't like it," Maddalena goes on, "we can give what you've left over to Tommasino and Amerigo, okay?"

"No!" Mariuccia bursts out, tears squeezing out of her eyes. Then she looks down at the ground and blushes. "Actually, I wanted to save a little for my brothers, when I get back home, and I wanted to hide it in the pocket of my dress."

"But you can't save ice cream; it melts!" Maddalena says.

"If it melts, how am I going to do the solidarity thing?"

Maddalena dips her hand into her bag and takes out five or six candies.

"Here you go; these are better for solidarity. You can keep them for your brothers."

Mariuccia holds the candies as if they were a string of diamonds and puts them in her pocket. Then, finally, she eats the last of her ice cream.

II

THE COMMUNIST SIGNORINAS SIT US ON LONG benches, in rows. They come by holding a black book, read the numbers on our shirtsleeves, ask us our names, and write them down in the book.

"Annichiaro, Maria?" a signorina asks Mariuccia, and she nods. The woman pins a red badge on Mariuccia's chest and turns to Tommasino.

"Saporito, Tommaso?"

"Present," he says, standing up as if he were answering the roll call at school.

The signorina ties his shoelaces, pins his badge, and moves on.

"I'm Speranza," I say, calling her back.

She turns, looks for my name in her ledger, and writes something down.

"What about the badge?" I ask as she is walking away.

"I've finished mine; another comrade will be coming, don't worry."

I wait and wait, but nobody else comes, and I'm beginning to get worried.

This is when the families from northern Italy start to file in. Some adults come in a gaggle with their kids, others come alone. There are both men and women. Then there are couples, husbands and wives with no children, who are the most excited, because it is as if they are coming to pick a kid of their own, exactly how they want it.

All the people from northern Italy, the men, the women, and the children, are bigger and fatter than we are, and their faces pink and white. Maybe because they've eaten so much of that ham with white spots. I think that if I stay here for a while, when I go home I'll be bigger and fatter, too, and I'm pretty sure Mamma Antonietta will say, "Weeds grow the fastest," because giving compliments is not her strong point.

The signorina with the black ledger comes along with a couple from the north, who stop in front of a little girl three places in front of me. She has long blond hair and blue eyes, and they pick her immediately. Nobody comes near me, maybe because I still have a melon head. The couple from the north hold the little blond girl's hand and lead her out of the room. The signorina then goes up to a plump woman with red hair. They wander around the room and stop in front of two girls with chestnut braids in the row right in front of me. Since they look alike, I think they must be sisters. In fact, the redheaded lady takes them both, holding both by the hand, one on each side.

Mariuccia, Tommasino, and I huddle close together, hoping they will take all three of us.

"Amerì," Tommasino says. "These people are from the north. They're not blind. Don't you think they can see we are not from the same family? You're a redhead, I'm black as pitch, and Mariuccia's hair is straw yellow. How could we possibly be brothers and sisters?"

Tommasino's right, and I feel confused. All the other kids are going off with their new parents, and we're still here. Nobody likes the coal-head, the evil-haired boy, or the scruffy, straw-haired tomboy.

As the room empties out, it gets bigger and colder. Every noise, even the softest sound, rumbles like thunder. I shift my weight on the bench and let out a fart. I'm so ashamed, I want to disappear. Mariuccia, Tommasino, and I don't dare say a word, so we start gesticulating. Tommasino forms a gun with his fingers and then shakes it, as if to say, "There's no room for us here." Mariuccia makes a fist and shakes it, as if to say, "What the heck are we doing up here." I shrug and open my hands, as if to say, "What do I know about it?" Then Tommasino raises his eyebrows and opens his hands, looking at me, "Weren't you supposed to be Nobèl?" "Yes, yes. I was Nobèl on my street, but I'm nobody up here," is what I'd like to say, but there are no gestures to express it, and so I pull in air with my nose and puff it out of my mouth like Capa 'e Fierro does when he's smoking.

Maddalena looks at us from a distance and starts gesturing, too. She puts an open hand up, as if to say, "Be patient, wait, it will be your turn soon." But I'm thinking of Mamma Antonietta's face when they send me back after nobody has picked me. She'll say, "So, you made a name for yourself even up in northern Italy, did you?" because consoling people is not her strong point either.

A young couple comes up to us, accompanied by one of the signorinas. They stop and look at us. The woman is wearing a headscarf, but I can see that underneath her hair is as black as Mamma's. She's neither tall nor fat, and her skin is dark. She looks over all three of us. Her coat is open, and I can see she's wearing a dress with a red flowery pattern on it.

"My mother has a housecoat that is the twin of your dress," I say, trying to butter her up. She doesn't understand me and turns her head the other way like the hen Pachiochia used to keep.

"Her housecoat . . ." I pick up again, but I feel less and less sure of myself. The signorina takes her arm, whispers something in her ear, and then leads her away to another group of kids.

Tommasino and Mariuccia are staring at me, but I don't dare lift my eyes from my brown laces. Before leaving, I thought I could go anywhere and do anything with new shoes. Instead, the shoes are tight, and I'm still here. Nobody wants me.

Maddalena is watching from the other side of the room. She goes up to two signorinas, and then all three turn and look at us. Maddalena points us out, one by one. The signorinas run around the room talking to people here and there, and finally a young couple, husband and wife, and an older man with a salt-and-pepper mustache, approach us. The young couple smiles at Mariuccia. The wife, who is really young and has blond hair the color of straw, reaches out and strokes Mariuccia's head. She feels the hard stubble of her hair starting to grow back and makes a sad face, as if it were Mariuccia's fault her father had shaved her head. She looks at her husband and then squats down to Mariuccia's level.

"Would you like to come home with us?"

Mariuccia doesn't know what to say. I give her a poke with my elbow, because if she doesn't open her mouth, they'll think she's deaf, as well as dirty, and then they won't pick her. So Mariuccia moves her head up and down slowly.

"What's your name?" the kind young wife asks, resting both her hands on Mariuccia's shoulders.

"Maria," Mariuccia says, to sound less Neapolitan.

"Maria. What a lovely name! Here you go, Maria. This is for you!" She puts a little tin in front of her with cookies, candies, and a little bead bracelet in it.

Mariuccia keeps her hands behind her back without speaking. The lady looks upset.

"Don't you like candies, Maria? Take them. They're yours . . ."

Mariuccia finally plucks up the courage and says, "I can't, ma'am. They told me that if I take my hands out from behind my back, they'll cut them off, and then how will I be able to help my father with the shoe repairs?"

The lady and her husband look at each other. Then the lady gets down on her knees and takes Mariuccia's hands, which were crossed behind her back, holding them tight.

"You don't need to worry. You are my daughter now. These little hands will be safe."

When Mariuccia hears "my daughter," she smiles for the first time since I met her. Then she reaches out and picks up the tin.

"Thank you, sir, thank you, ma'am," she says. "But why did you get me a present? It's not my name day."

The couple look at each other again, a question mark written in their eyebrows. Luckily, Maddalena is there and she tells them that back home, Mariuccia would receive little gifts only on her feast day.

Mariuccia is flushed with embarrassment and she grabs the young wife's hand just in case the couple changes their mind. But the young wife hasn't changed her mind. The opposite: her heart has melted.

"I'll give you lots of presents, my lovely daughter, you'll see! You'll get so many, you won't even remember when your saint's day is!"

Mariuccia grips the kind lady's hand and won't let go. Either because she's worried that she won't remember her name day anymore, or because the blond lady reminds her of her mamma, bless her soul. Who knows? Anyway, she opens and closes her fingers to wave *ciao* and goes off with the young couple. Me and Tommasino are the last kids in the room.

The man with the salt-and-pepper mustache comes up to Tommasino and holds out his hand.

"I'm Libero, it's a pleasure to meet you!" he says, as if he were kidding.

"I'm free, too," Tommasino says, unsure what he is supposed to do. Then he sticks his hand out and the two shake hands. The man with the mustache doesn't understand the joke, but goes along anyway.

"Would this nice tanned young man like to come with me?"

"Is there a lot of work involved?" Tommasino asked.

"No, the automobile is just outside. It'll take no longer than half an hour."

"Automobile? Are you a cab driver?"

"Come, now . . . I could see from the start that this boy likes a good joke. He has a sense of humor, this one! Come along now, Gina is waiting for us with hot food on the table . . ."

As soon as Tommasino hears the words *hot, food,* and *table* he makes up his mind on the spot and slips away like an eel.

"Bye, Amerì. *Arrivederci!* Good Luck!"

"See you soon, Tommasino. Take care . . ."

12

Tommasino has gone, too, and I'm left alone on the wooden bench, my tight shoes pinching my feet and sadness filling my belly. My eyes are pricking. It's like there's a needle behind my eyes holding my tears one by one, and if one drops, they will all unthread like a beaded necklace. When we were all together in the train, with all the kids laughing, blubbering, or running around, I felt as strong as my American father. As long as Mariuccia and Tommasino were there, scared to death, I could act strong, joshing with them and talking. I was still Nobèl. But now I feel like that day when I was biting into a pork-fat-and-pepper *tarallo* cracker and I felt a terrible pain in my mouth. I fished out my tooth, all covered in blood, and ran to Mamma Antonietta, but she was locked in with Capa 'e Fierro and couldn't talk to me. So I went to Zandragliona's house, and she sat me down in my usual chair and rinsed my mouth out with water mixed with a sachet of Idrolitina, bicarbonate of soda and lemon, to disinfect everything and explained how I would lose all my milk teeth one after another, just as they had grown one after another when I was a baby, and that my big teeth would soon grow in to replace them.

Well, that's how I feel now. Like a tooth that has fallen out. Where the tooth used to be, there is a big gap, but the new tooth isn't there yet.

I look around to see whether the lady in the red flowery dress has changed her mind and is coming to get me. Maybe she wanted to look at all the kids before choosing. As Zandragliona always says when we go shopping, "Never stop at the first stall!" In fact, we would always go around all the vegetable stalls to see who had the freshest produce. Zandragliona would stop in front of a basket of melons, touch them, smell them, prod the skin with her thumb to see if it was ripe or not. Maybe you can do the same thing with kids? Prod them to see if they're good or bad inside.

The lady with the red flowery dress and her husband have done one round of the whole hall, accompanied by the signorina with the black ledger, as if they were looking for someone in particular. I sit up straight on the bench, practically holding my breath. She doesn't look like Mamma after all. I thought she did because she wasn't smiling either. It looks like they're heading for the exit. They must have changed their mind: none of the fruit was fresh enough. But then the signorina with the black ledger leads them to a corner where there is the gap-toothed blond boy. I didn't realize he was still here; I thought I was the only one left. From a distance, I can see the signorina reading the number pinned to his sleeve. The boy isn't even looking at them. He stares down at his nails, which are now as black as they were before they made us have a shower. The husband says something to the boy, but he doesn't answer. He moves his head up and down as if he were doing them a favor, not the other way around. As he gets up and follows them out of the hall he turns and grins at me with a mean face as if to say, "They took me even though I didn't tell them my name, and nobody's taking you."

The couple have made quite a bargain! If Zandragliona had been here, she would have discarded that melon for sure . . . but the truth is that he's right. I'm the only one nobody wants.

Maddalena looks at me from the other side of the room as she talks to a lady in a gray skirt, a white blouse, and a coat. She must be the one who takes the discarded kids back home, because she's wearing a badge with the Communist flag on it, and she looks strict and serious. Her hair is blond, but not like Zandragliona's; it's a more delicate, pale yellow. The lady is listening to her, but she doesn't move. She doesn't even turn around to look when Maddalena points at me. Then she nods her head a few times as if to say, "Yes, yes, I'll take care of this one." Then they both walk to me. I force my feet back into my shoes, straighten my jacket, and stand up.

"My name is Derna," the lady says.

"Amerigo Speranza," I answer, holding out my hand like Tommasino did with the salt-and-pepper-mustached man. She holds it, but doesn't squeeze it.

I can see talking is not her strong point. She just wants to get on with it and go home. Maddalena gives me a kiss on the forehead and says goodbye.

"Be good, Amerì. I'm leaving you in good hands."

"Let's go, son. It's getting late," the lady says, grabbing my arm and pulling me. "We'll miss the bus if we don't hurry."

We hurry away, me and the lady, like thieves running away from the police. We walk close together, at the same pace, not too fast and not too slow, and soon find ourselves outside the train station. There's an enormous square in front of us, with red brick buildings and lots of trees.

"Where are we?" I ask, a little dazed.

"This city is called Bologna. It's a nice city, but we need to go home now.

"Are you taking me home with you, signorina?"

"Of course I am, son."

"Don't we need to go on a train?"

"It's quicker on the bus."

AT THE BUS STOP I START SHAKING.

"Are you cold?"

I feel shivers running up and down my spine, but I don't know whether it's the cold or my fear. The lady opens her coat wide and lets me come inside.

"With this cold and damp weather, they send them up here with no coats. My God . . ."

I don't say anything about throwing our coats out the train window, or about the mothers giving them to their other children. I just think about my mother's face when she sees I've been sent back like the discards from the vegetable market. I plunge my hands deep into my jacket pockets and that's when I realize Mamma's apple is still there. I pull it out, but I can't bring myself to eat it. My stomach is in knots.

"One adult, one child," the lady says to the ticket man when the bus comes. We climb on and sit side by side. The new shoes are hurting. It feels like I've been wearing them for a whole year, not just one day. The bus leaves. It's getting dark and my eyes are drooping. Before falling asleep, I slip my shoes off under the seat and leave them there. What use are they, anyway? I was barefoot when I left, and I'll be barefoot when I get sent back.

Part Two

13

WHEN I OPEN MY EYES, IT'S PITCH BLACK. I stretch my feet out to feel for Mamma Antonietta's legs and look around to where the light usually filters in through the half-closed shutters. I sit up in the middle of the empty bed, and there is no relief from the dark. I fumble around the room with my arms stretched out and my hands like scoopers looking for a window, a door, anything to orient myself with.

"Mamma! Mamma!" I start shouting.

There is no answer. The silence tells me I'm not home on my street.

"Mamma," I call again, more softly.

The darkness is wrapped around me, and I'm not sure whether I'm awake or asleep. My heart is beating hard, and I can't remember a thing. I was on a bus with a blond lady, who was supposed to be taking me back home. I must have fallen asleep, and now I've woken up in this strange bed.

After a while, I hear a sound coming closer and closer. A door opens. It's not Mamma Antonietta; it's the lady who came to get me yesterday.

"Did you have a bad dream?"

Without the gray skirt and white blouse, she looks less like a Communist.

"I don't know. I can't remember."

"Would you like a glass of water? I'm going to the kitchen . . ."

I don't answer. She crosses her arms over her breast and rubs her shoulders to warm herself up and walks toward the door.

"Signorina," I call out to her. "Have you brought me to Russia?"

She opens her arms wide.

"Russia? Poor little boy. What did they tell you down there? No wonder you had bad dreams. These stories are enough to give you nightmares!"

I feel as though I've made her angry, but it's hard to tell in the dark because I can't see her face. The lady comes back to my bedside and brushes my cheek with her hand, which is cool to the touch.

"We're in Modena, not Russia, with people who will grow fond of you. This is home. Trust me . . ."

This isn't home and Mamma always says not to trust anyone, I think. But I don't say anything.

"I'll go and get you some water," she says.

"Signorina," I murmur as she is about to vanish into the darkness.

"What is it, son? You must call me Derna, though. I've told you . . ."

"Don't go, please. I'm scared . . ."

"I'll leave the door open, so there's a little light," she says, disappearing behind the door.

I am alone in the room. It's so dark it makes no difference whether my eyes are open or closed. After a while, the lady comes back with a glass of water.

"You can drink it, son. Don't worry, we haven't poisoned the wells. Is that what they told you?" she asks, as if she were angry.

"No, no, of course they didn't," I say, trying to appease her. "Sorry, it's just because Mamma always tells me to sip my water slowly, so I don't get indigestion."

The lady looks upset, as if she's lost face somehow.

"I'm sorry, son," she says, in a kinder voice. "You drew the short straw with me. I don't really understand kids. I don't have any of my own. My cousin Rosa is good with them. She has three."

"Don't worry, *signò*," I reassure her. "My mother had two, but kids are not her strong point, either."

"So, you have a brother?"

"No, ma'am! I'm an only child."

The lady doesn't say anything. Maybe she's still upset about the poisoned water.

"Tomorrow morning we'll go to meet her kids. Kids need to be with kids, not with signorinas, as you call them."

I'm embarrassed, because I still can't bring myself to call her by name.

"You'll like them, they're almost your age . . . How old are you? I didn't even ask. You see what a warm welcome I've given you. You must excuse me . . ."

The lady is asking *me* to excuse *her*. When I should be asking her to excuse me for being here in her house, eating and drinking, sleeping in her bed, and waking her up in the middle of the night.

"I'll be eight next month," I tell her. "Anyhow, I'm not scared of the dark. One time I was locked inside a chapel with some live skeletons!"

"You're a brave boy; you're lucky. You're not scared of anything."

"Well, one thing . . ."

"That I'll take you to Russia?"

"No, ma'am! I never believed the stories about Russia . . ."

"I've actually been to Russia, you know? With some companions from the Party."

"I've never been anywhere, and I've never had companions. This is the first time. That's why I'm scared."

"It's only natural . . . all these changes . . ."

"No, ma'am! The truth is, I'm not used to sleeping alone. At home, there was only one bed: for me, for Mamma, and for Capa 'e Fierro's coffee stash before the police took him away. But don't tell anyone or Mamma will kill me. It's a secret."

She sits on the bed beside me. She smells different from Mamma. Sweeter.

"I'll tell you a secret, too. When the mayor asked us to take a child in, I said no. I was scared."

"Are you scared of kids?"

"No, I was scared I wouldn't know how to console them. I know about politics, about labor relations, and a little about Latin. But I don't know anything about kids," she says, staring at a fixed spot on the wall like Mamma always does when she's doing the talking. "I've become a bit brusque over the years."

"But you did take me."

"I came to the station to lend a hand and make sure everything went smoothly. Then Comrade Criscuolo told me there had been a problem with the couple that was supposed to take you. The wife had been rushed into the hospital because her baby had come early, so there was no one to come and pick you up."

"So that's why I was the last one there!"

"When I saw you sitting there on the bench all alone, with your lovely red hair and those cute little freckles, I decided I would take you. I don't know if I did the right thing. Maybe you would have preferred a real family?"

"I don't know. The only thing I have ever preferred is my mother."

The lady strokes my hand. Her fingers are cold and chapped. She hardly ever smiles, but she did take me home with her.

"I thought I was the only one left because nobody wanted me."

"No, son. Everything was organized. We worked on it for weeks. Every child had a family to go to."

"You mean they didn't choose the ones they wanted?"

"Of course not. It's not like a fruit-and-vegetable market!"

I'm embarrassed because that's exactly what I'd thought it was.

"Now we need to get to sleep, though. I'm working tomorrow. You know what I'll do?" she says. "I'll lie here right beside you. Here we go. Is that okay?" The lady lies down beside me. I don't know whether it's okay or not, but I scoot over and make room for her on my pillow.

"Shall I sing you a lullaby? Would you like that, eh?"

Lullabies make me feel sad in my belly but I don't tell the lady, so that she doesn't get angry with me again.

"Yes," I say, with my eyes closed and a foot touching her leg. I really hope it's not going to be the one about the bogeyman, though. The one where he keeps the child for a whole year. Because if it is, I'm pretty sure I'll start crying, and tomorrow they'll put me straight back onto the train and send me home. The lady thinks for a while, and then she starts singing the song we heard when we arrived at the station. The one where they sing *"bella ciao ciao ciao"* every other line.

When the song comes to an end, I don't say a word for a while, and then I ask, *"Signò*, do you mind my cold feet on your leg?"

"Not at all, son. Not at all."

I slowly drift off to sleep. Finally.

14

"Amerì," a voice calls, "Amerigo, wake up! Your brother Luigi's coming back. Hurry, hurry! Get out of bed. This is his place!"

My eyes tight shut, I say, "What about me? Where am I supposed to go?"

"You?" Mamma Antonietta answers. "You're up there now, with the lady . . ."

When I open my eyes, it's morning. Through the window opposite the bed I can see brown fields and frozen trees, with skeleton branches and a few dry leaves left hanging there. There are no other houses. Nobody walks by, and I can't hear a single voice outside.

The lady is in the kitchen at the end of the corridor. I watch her from the door as she makes breakfast and listens to the radio. I'd only ever seen radios in rich people's houses when they gave me rags to take away. On the table there's a big cup of milk, a thick chunk of bread, a jar of red jam, a slab of butter, and a big hunk of cheese. I wonder whether Tommasino woke up to all these good things in the house of the man with the salt-and-pepper mustache. The lady has also set the table with a knife, a fork, a teaspoon, and cups and saucers in a set, all the same color.

She's wearing the gray skirt and white blouse again. She still hasn't spotted me. I'd like to call out, but I'm embarrassed. She looks different than last night. On the radio, a man's voice is speaking fast. I catch the words *children, hospitality, disease, Communist Party, south, poverty.* The man is talking about me. The lady stops cutting slices of bread to listen and sighs, puffing out all the air she has kept inside her at once, like Capa 'e Fierro, except without the smoke rings. Then she starts slicing again.

After a while, she turns around and looks surprised to see me.

"Ah, here you are. I didn't hear you. I've got something ready. I don't know whether you like it or not."

"I like everything."

We eat together in silence. The lady only really talks at night; during the day she doesn't say much. Anyway, I'm used to it. Chatting isn't Mamma Antonietta's strong point, either. Especially first thing in the morning.

When we've finished our breakfast, the lady tells me she has to go to work, but she says she's not leaving me on my own. She's taking me to her cousin Rosa's house, the one with the three children, and then she'll pick me up when she's done. I'm thinking that I've just arrived and I'm already being moved on, and my belly is churning again. Mamma Antonietta handed me over to Maddalena, Maddalena handed me over to Signora Derna, and now Signora Derna is handing me over to her cousin Rosa. Who knows who this Rosa lady is going to hand me over to? It's just like the lullaby about the bogeyman.

I go with the lady into the room where I slept. You can't see the sky or the fields or the trees anymore. I try to wipe the window with my hand, but nothing changes. It's not the glass that's dirty. It's the air. There's a pall of smoke covering everything. I sit on the edge of the bed.

"Do you want me to help you get dressed?" the lady asks.

I can't see the clothes I arrived in anywhere. There's the apple Mamma gave me, that I had in my pocket, sitting on the desk, though.

"I can get dressed on my own, thank you," I answer.

She takes some clothes out of a brown wooden wardrobe. Woolen sweaters, shirts, pants. They belonged to her cousin Rosa's oldest boy, and now they're going to be mine. I tell her they look new. On the desk, there are some notebooks and a pen. She says I'll soon be going to school.

"Again?" I say. "I've already been there once!"

"That's why you need to go. Every day. You couldn't have learned everything, right?"

"No one is born knowing everything!" I say, and, for the first time since we've been together, we burst out laughing.

I look at myself in the mirror in my new clothes and see a boy who looks like me, but isn't me. The lady buttons up my coat and puts a hat on my head.

"Wait," she says, going into the other room.

She comes back with a little badge in her hand. It's red with a yellow half-circle in the middle and a picture of a hammer, just like hers. She sits down next to me and pins it on the lapel of my coat. The image is the same as the flags I saw in the Communist headquarters in Via Medina. That must mean they've made me into a Communist. I have a sudden flash of the sad, blond young man and wonder whether he ever solved that terrible "problem of the south."

"Are we ready?" the lady asks as she puts her hat on.

"*Sì, Signò* . . . no, sorry, I mean . . . yes, Derna."

The lady makes a face as if she's just won a straight five-in-a-row at the lottery.

We step out and walk hand in hand. Her steps are not as fast as Mamma Antonietta's. She doesn't leave me one step behind. Or maybe it's me walking faster, because I'm scared of being left on my own in the smoky gray air.

15

"They smoke a lot up here, don't they? You can't even see the street."

"It's not smoke; it's fog. Are you scared?"

"No. I like it when things are hiding and then they come out all of a sudden, like a surprise."

"This is my cousin Rosa's house. When the weather is nice, you can see it from our window, but the fog makes it disappear."

"I'd like to disappear every now and again, but down south we don't have fog yet."

Derna rings the doorbell with a name on it.

"What does it say?" I ask.

"Benvenuti," she answers.

"Did they write it to welcome us?" I ask.

"No! It's my brother-in-law's name," she answers, trying not to laugh.

A boy with shoulder-length brown hair opens the door. His eyes are bright blue and he has a little gap between his two front teeth. He gives Derna a hug and then turns and does the same to me.

"You're the kid that came on the train. I've never been on a train. What's it like?"

"Crowded," I say.

"That jacket isn't yours. My brother wore it last winter," another boy says as he runs toward us along the corridor. He's the same height as me and his eyes are black.

"Mine, yours . . . what's the difference? It belongs to the person that needs it," a tall, thin man with a reddish mustache and blue eyes scolds. "Rosa, you're not bringing up our boy as a Fascist, I hope."

"Well done, boys. That was a nice way to welcome this poor child, who's already been through enough in his life," the wife says, carrying a baby. She gestures that I should follow her into the living room.

"We haven't even introduced ourselves. I'm Rosa, Derna's cousin; the joker over there with the mustache is Alcide, and these are our three boys: Rivo, who's ten, Luzio, who's turning seven, and Nario, who isn't even one yet.

Their names are hard to understand, and they have to repeat them three times before I learn them. Where I come from, we have names like Giuseppe, Salvatore, Mimmo, Annunziata, or Linuccia. And then we have nicknames like Zandragliona, Pachiochia, Capajanca, Naso 'e Cane . . . after a while nobody remembers what their real names are. Take Capa 'e Fierro, for example. If you asked me what his first and last names were, I wouldn't have the faintest idea.

Up here, it's different. Their father says he invented the names himself. They're not in the calendar of saints because, for one thing, he doesn't believe in saints. He believes in calendars, he says, but not in God. He says that he chose these names because he is a revolutionary, and when he calls his three kids together it spells *Rivo-Luzio-Nario*! When he says this, he looks at me, waiting. I look back and realize he's expecting a reaction from me. Then he starts laughing out loud on his own, his mustache twitching. In the street where I live, nobody has a mustache, except Pachiochia but she's not a man, so she doesn't count. To please him, I start laughing too, though I don't get what the big joke is. I'm just pretending, and I hope he doesn't notice.

Derna says she's going to work, and she'll pick me up this evening. Rosa's husband leaves too. He has to go to an important person's house. It's a rich family, and all the kids study music at the Conservatory, which is why he's going to tune their piano. As soon as I hear the word *Conservatory*, I blurt out: "I went to the Conservatory, too, when I was back home in the south!"

Alcide looks at me, his mustache suddenly still and serious.

"What instrument do you play, then?"

I feel my face blushing a hot red.

"No instrument, Don Alcide. I used to go to the Conservatory . . . from the outside. To listen to the music. I've never been inside. I used to wait for my friend there. . . . She really did play an instrument. I mean, she played in the Conservatory. Her name's Carolina, and she says I have a musical ear."

He looks at me, stroking his mustache.

"Do you know the notes?"

I say I do.

"All seven?" he asks.

I recite all seven of them, from *do* to *ti*. Carolina taught me. He looks happy and puts a hand on my shoulder. He says that sometimes after school I can come with him to the piano shop.

"Will I be allowed to touch the keys?" I ask.

"None of my children have shown any interest in music. Lucky you arrived, right, Rosa?"

Luzio scowls at me as if to say, "Look what's just arrived fresh on our doorstep."

"If you're a good little helper, I'll give you some pocket money," the boy's father says.

"I've been getting pocket money for over a year," Rivo boasts. "I work in the cow pen and give the cows water."

"And you stink of cow shit," his younger brother teases.

"We all work here, to each his own," their father says.

"Don Alcide," I say, "I used to go and collect rags with my friend Tommasino, but I'm much happier working with pianos. At least I won't be getting a bald patch on my head."

The man tugs at his reddish mustache and then holds out his hand.

"Agreed, then? I've found an assistant. But you need to stop calling me Don. I'm not a priest, you know!"

Luzio snickers.

"Whatever you wish," I say. "So . . . what should I call you?"

"You can call me Babbo," he answers brusquely.

Luzio stops snickering, and I am just as shocked.

16

"B YE, BABBO, SEE YOU THIS EVENING!"
Rivo walks to the door with his father and gives him a kiss. Luzio takes a marble out of his pocket and rolls it down the corridor. I wave bye-bye without saying a word. I can't bring myself to call him Babbo. I've been told this is how people here say "Dad" but to me it feels like a joke. On my street there was this big fat man and every time we bumped into him, Tommasino and I would chant: "*Babbasòne, babbasò*, you look just like a rum baba!" Alcide doesn't look like a *babà*, so how am I supposed to call him Babbo? Anyhow, he's not even my father.

Rosa has to go out to pick dandelion leaves in the field. Rivo fetches a pail of water for the cows. He says they have a vegetable plot, too, and a few animals, though there are only a few hens left, and he also says that he's learning to milk the cows, but that you need to do it delicately. Rivo knows so many things and he wants to explain them all to me at the same time. Water, fertilizer, the milk that comes out of the cows, the cheese they make out of the milk that comes out of the cows.

The animals are not just theirs; they keep them together with other families, and they all contribute their work. They eat some of what they produce and take the rest to market. I wanted to tell him that I went to the market, too, with Tommasino to sell sewer rats, but Rivo isn't listening. He starts talking again, pulling on his boots and donning his jacket to go work outside with the animals.

He asks me if I want to come. I don't answer. Pachiochia was right, I'm thinking, they brought us up north to put us to work.

"Rivo, you'll drive him crazy with your chitter-chatter. Leave him alone for a while. He needs to get used to us slowly. He's just arrived! You see, Amerigo, this boy is made of quicksilver."

"What does that mean?"

"It means he can't stay still or quiet for a second."

"I get it. Like when Mamma says I was sent by God to punish her."

Rivo bursts out laughing, and so do I. Luzio doesn't even smile. He goes on playing with the marble. Rosa picks us some shoes full of mud and opens the door.

"Luzio, if your brother wakes up, come and call me."

She goes out and then comes back in again.

"And give one of your marbles to our new friend here. That way you can play together."

When we are left on our own, Luzio hides the marble in his pocket and goes off. I look all over for him, but I can't find him. Either he's hiding or he's made himself invisible, even though there's no fog inside the house. The rooms are big, and there are sausages and whole sides of ham hanging from the beams on the kitchen ceiling, like at the grocer's in Via Foria. It's the warmest room in the house because there's a fire lit in the fireplace. That's why Rosa left the baby here in its crib. From a faraway place in the house, I hear the sound of a marble rolling on the floor. One, two, three . . . I start counting on my fingers, so that when I get to ten times ten something nice will happen, like the other brother, the one who talks a lot, will come back and show me the animals. Time goes by, the fire is burning low and then it goes out altogether. And I can't even hear the sound of a marble rolling. I look out the window to see whether anyone is coming, but the fog is still thick.

"Luzio," I call out feebly, but he either can't hear or doesn't want to answer. In the corner of the kitchen, half-hidden behind the dresser, there's a ladder. I pull it out and lean it against the wall. I've never been up a ladder. Pachiochia says it brings bad luck if you walk under one. I put one foot on the first rung to see if it holds my weight, then the next, and the next, and before I know it, I'm up high, feeling big and strong, and I forget they've left me on my own again. I climb up to the top, because I want to touch the ceiling. Stretching out my fingers, I feel the warm rough-hewn beams. The hanging salamis rub against my face, their smell going up my nose and making my mouth water. I've never seen such an array of goods: there's even the big mortadella sausage with white spots they gave us in Bologna. I scratch away at its skin with my nail until I get down to the tender pink flesh. I bore in farther with my finger, and then pull it out and suck on it. I go back to the hole and do it again. When the hole is too deep, I start drilling another, and then another.

"Thief!" I hear from somewhere below me. "You've come here to steal all our stuff."

I turn on my heels and lose my balance, falling off the ladder. It's not very far but I fall on my back painfully. The baby in the crib wakes up and starts crying. Luzio glares at me and then gazes up at the ceiling and sees the holes in the mortadella sausage. He pokes me with the toe of his shoe as he would an insect to see whether it's dead or alive. I don't move. I don't even say "ouch." He runs off. Nario is still crying. I'm scared Rosa will come in right now and think I've done something wrong.

"Luzio," I call out, still lying on the floor. "I didn't even want to come here. It was my mother who sent me. It was for my own good and I pretended to be a stuttering, dribbling idiot, but they still took me . . ."

He doesn't answer. I can hear the marble rolling. It's near; maybe in the next room.

"I just wanted a taste, and anyway, what do you care? You have everything: animals in their pens, salamis hanging from the ceiling, a father with a mustache, woolen sweaters in your wardrobes. You even have photographs on the wall."

He still doesn't answer. I pull myself into a sitting position on the floor. My back is hurting but it's bearable. I crawl over to the crib and rock it like I saw a neighbor of Zandragliona's do with her little baby, and Nario slowly stops crying and falls asleep again. The sound of the marble is getting closer and closer, and finally I see it rolling through the door, followed by Luzio.

"Who's that bald man inside the frame over there? Is he your godfather?"

"That's Comrade Lenin," he says, without looking at me.

"Is he a friend of your father's?" I ask.

"He's everyone's friend. Babbo says he taught us about communism."

"Nobody is born knowing everything," I conclude. Then we sit in silence again. The fire is almost all embers, and it's getting a little cold. Luzio gets up, picks a log from the woodpile, and puts it in the fireplace. The fire soon starts burning again, stronger than before, and the flames are moving again. I'd like to know how to get a fire going, I think.

"There's a friend of mine, her name's Pachiochia," I say, acting indifferent. "She has a portrait in her house, too, but it's not a picture of her dead fiancé, bless his soul. It's the king with a mustache. She brought it with her when she came with a procession to try and stop us leaving: maybe she was right, after all."

Luzio doesn't say a word and makes as if to leave again.

"I'm not staying here forever, you know. They said it was just to get through the winter. So, when I leave, you can go and be your father's assistant, and I'll be going back where I came from. That way, everything will go back to how it was before, thank God."

I stick my hand out like I've seen adults do when they've just made a business deal. Luzio doesn't shake it, but with a kick he rolls the marble toward me. Then he puts the ladder back where it was, behind the dresser, and walks out of the kitchen. The marble is still on the floor. I'm not sure whether he's left it there on purpose or whether he's just forgotten it. I pick it up, stick it into my pocket, and carry on staring at the fire flickering in the grate.

17

SINCE NOBODY COMES BACK, I DECIDE TO GO
out into the field. Rivo sees me and runs to greet me, grabbing my hand. I think about the holes in the mortadella and feel hot with shame, but I follow him into the cow pen.

"The cow is easy to deal with, but when the bull has his funny five minutes, it's best to keep out of his way," Rivo tells me. I look the bull in the face and I can see he has a nasty temper, a bit like Mamma Antonietta, who is sweet and nice, but when you get in her way, she literally sees red.

I'd never seen animals that big before. Well, I'd never really seen any animals for that matter. Except for Ciccio Cheese, as we used to call him. So I ended up telling the two brothers about the alley cat that used to hang around outside Zandragliona's; she would always give a crust of bread and a bowl of milk to him. When Mamma Antonietta saw him, she would call him "Magnapane" behind his back, and she would always send him running with a kick in the backside. Cats are not her strong point. Tommasino and I always used to say he was ours, and that we were training him, because we'd seen an old man on the Corso with a trained monkey. The old man said "sit," and the monkey sat. The old man said "stand up," and the monkey stood up. The old man said "dance," and the monkey danced. People stopped to stare and dropped coins in his hat. The old man and the monkey made a lot of money, especially in front of the wealthy apartment buildings. When the show was over, the old man would pick up the monkey, and they would go on their way. The next day, he was there again in another spot. Tommasino and I went around town looking for him. First, because we had never seen a live monkey in our lives. Second, because we wanted to find out how to make the monkey do the things he did.

One day, the old man vanished, and we never saw him again. That's how we had the idea of training Ciccio Cheese, the alley cat. Except that Ciccio Cheese had no intention whatsoever of being trained. He only wanted to do what he wanted to do. Mamma Antonietta was not that wrong, in the end. But he was still our cat. We stroked him, and he would rub himself up against our legs. When he saw us come up the alley, he would run toward us, his tail swishing.

But then Ciccio Cheese vanished, too. We looked high and low for him, but we couldn't find him. I told Tommasino that maybe he'd gone off with the old man to be trained and live the good life with lots of money. Pachiochia said people were so hungry that they would eat cats. I didn't believe her. But the truth is that Ciccio Cheese had gotten nice and fat thanks to Zandragliona's bread and milk, so somebody might have decided to eat him after all.

Rivo doesn't let me finish my story. He says the cat will come back. That's the way animals are. Every now and again, they disappear, but then they always find their way home.

"I like dogs. Do you?"

I like cats. Because, sooner or later, I'll find my way home too.

Rivo goes up to the cow.

"Come," he says. "She won't hurt you."

He starts stroking the cow's forehead, right between her two horns. The cow doesn't even swish her tail. I think she'd be impossible to train. Then Rivo calls me over.

"Pet her!" he says.

I reach out my arm and touch her with the tips of my fingers. Her fur isn't as soft as Ciccio Cheese's, and, as I get close, she smells of old feet. I come even closer and pat her with my whole hand. Her eyes are watery and her muzzle is turned down like Mamma Antonietta's mouth that day when we left the Communist headquarters and she offered to buy me a slice of fried pizza.

18

I DON'T WANT TO WEAR THE SCHOOL SMOCK THAT looks like a girl's dress, nor the white bow that goes on the collar. It's embarrassing. But Derna looks happy, so I don't say anything. She acts like she's getting me ready for a party, but what I'm going to be getting are whacks around the ears, the smell of sweat, and rows of straight lines to copy into my schoolbook.

"I know my numbers already," I tell her. "I can count to ten times ten on my fingers!"

"Well, you need to learn your letters, too. And long division. And geography."

"I hate letters. Mamma never knew them, so why should I? What's the point?"

"Not to get cheated by people who know them. That's the point. Come on, let's go."

She takes me by the hand and we go out. There's no fog this morning, and I can see Rivo and Luzio with their black smocks sticking out under their jackets and a bag across their shoulders like mine. Rivo runs up to me and tells me the cow is expecting. There's a baby calf on the way. Luzio lags behind and kicks a stone along the road with the toes of his shoes.

"Is there room for me in this new school?" I ask.

"There aren't any desks free in my class," Luzio says, looking down at the road.

"I spoke to the principal yesterday," Derna says. "You'll be in the same class as Luzio. You may be a year older, but you're a little behind. You should be happy because you'll be with the family even when you're at school."

Luzio kicks the stone again and runs ahead to catch up with it. Derna says goodbye, because she has to go to a union meeting.

"Be sure to do a good job today, son."

She starts walking away, but then turns heel.

"Amerigo, wait! What an idiot I am! I forgot your snack."

It makes me think of Mamma's apple sitting on the desk. Derna runs back to me and pulls out of her bag a bundled-up tea cloth that releases a smell of lemon cake. I put it in my satchel and walk off with Rivo.

"We need to give the new calf a name," Rivo says. "What would you like to call it?"

I think Luigi would be nice, like my brother with bronchial asthma, but I don't get around to saying it, because Luzio is running to catch up with us, shouting, "It's my turn. I'm choosing the calf's name this time. One each, we said. This is my calf."

Rivo gives Luzio a shove, steals his stone, and gives it a big kick right up to the school door. I try running alongside him, but my smock is so long, my legs get twisted up in it, so I get there last.

In this school the teacher is a man and his name is Mr. Ferrari.

He's young, has no mustache, and can't pronounce his r's. He tells everyone I'm one of the train children, and that they should welcome me and make me feel at home. Which makes me think that I had nothing back home. Which means it would be better if they made me feel at their home, not mine.

Luzio sits at the front of the class, next to a tubby little blond boy with wavy hair. The only free place is right at the back. I sit there and wait for time to go by, but time goes by very slowly. Mr. Ferrari says, "Take your squared notebook," and everybody takes their squared notebook. Then he says, "Take your lined notebook," and everyone takes their lined notebook. Nobody needs any whacks in this class. They're all trained already, like the old man's monkey on Via Foria. At one point, the bell rings and I think, Thank God it's over. I put my jacket on and go toward the door. Everyone bursts out laughing. I don't get it, but I go back to my place. The teacher says it's recess, and we can eat our snack. The kids get up and talk. I remember my tea-cloth bundle and take the lemon cake out. Sitting in the back row on my own, I eat it slowly to pass the time. At the school I went to before, with the whacks around the ears, there was no recess and no lemon cake, and when the bell rang it meant one thing and one thing only: the beatings were over for the day.

Mr. Ferrari tells us recess is over and the kids all sit down.

"Let's repeat the two times table. Benvenuti, come to the blackboard."

Luzio stands up, gets a piece of chalk, writes the numbers, and then stands there like a stockfish staring at the board.

"Benvenuti, back to your place," the teacher says, a little annoyed but without lashing out at him.

"Who knows what two times seven is?"

Silence. Then Luzio says, "Ask Speranza."

"Speranza is new," the teacher says. "He's just arrived. He's still getting used to us."

"It'll make him feel at home," Luzio says. Some of the kids chuckle, and some of the kids turn around and look at me.

The teacher is a little uncertain. He smiles at me. You can see he's never given anyone a whack in his life.

"Speranza, do you know what two times seven makes?"

I can feel all the eyes in the class on me, and my voice is echoing around the room.

"It makes fourteen, sir."

Luzio glares at me with the same expression he had when he caught me boring holes into the mortadella, as if I had stolen something. Mr. Ferrari looks amazed but happy.

"Good boy, Speranza. Had you already studied the two times table back in your city?"

"No, sir," I answered. "Back in my city I counted shoes, which always come in pairs."

When the end-of-school bell rings and it's time to go home, the teacher tells us to hold hands until we get out. I stay on my own at the back of the class. Then one of the boys who was sitting at the front comes and takes my hand.

"*Am chièm Uliano,*" he says. I nod, but I don't say anything, because I'm fine with the two times table, but foreign languages are not my strong point.

19

THE SALAMIS ARE STILL HANGING IN THE kitchen, but the mortadella with my finger holes in it has gone. Nobody has said anything about it. If Mamma Antonietta had been here, she would have chased me down the street with a carpet beater. They don't give punishments here, but it's much worse because you never know how things will turn out. Last night I dreamed that someone was knocking at the door, and it was the police coming to get me. They threw me in jail with Capa 'e Fierro, who said, "They arrested me for the coffee and you for the mortadella. There's no difference, see?" In my dream I kept saying, "No, no, I'm not the same as you!" But when I woke up, I wasn't so sure anymore.

I get back from school, and I hear Don Alcide singing at the top of his voice, *"Nessun dorma! Nessun dormaaa . . ."* Let no one sleep. He often sings famous opera arias, but this time I think he has it in for me. I try to hide but he sees me anyway.

"Where are you going, young man? Do you have nothing to report?"

I stick my hands in my pockets and find Luzio's marble. I twizzle it around in my fingers and don't answer.

"I've heard something about you, but I'd like to hear it from you."

"Don Alcide, if I confess, do you promise you won't do anything?"

"Me? What am I supposed to do, son?"

"And you won't call the police?"

"Police? Nobody's ever been arrested for a good mark at school."

I take my hands out of my pockets.

"Ah, so you spoke to Mr. Ferrari?"

"He told me you're good with numbers and that you're trying hard with your letters."

"I like numbers more, because they never end."

"That must be why you love music, then. To play an instrument you need to be good at counting."

When I talk to Alcide, I never know whether he's joking or not. He goes up to the sideboard, takes a slice of mortadella, and cuts it in two.

"So, you're not angry with me?"

"A little, yes. Because you keep calling me Don Alcide and you haven't started calling me Babbo."

He cuts two slices of bread, puts the mortadella in the middle, and wraps the sandwiches in a tea cloth.

"One for me and one for you. Let's go!"

The workshop smells of wood and glue. There are instruments everywhere, some whole, some in pieces waiting to be put together again.

"What am I supposed to do?" I ask.

"Sit and watch," he says, and starts working. He cuts, hammers and files, explaining his every move to me. I listen and observe, and time flies. Not like at school. Alcide doesn't talk much while he's working. He says he needs to concentrate. "Listen!" he'll say, every now and again, plucking a string or touching a key. Then he pulls a metal fork out of his waistcoat pocket, taps it on the piano, and then rests it on the sounding board. The sound is like a ship blowing its horn as it leaves the port, from far away.

"I can play that instrument," I say. "It's easy."

"It's called a tuning fork. It only makes one note, but you use it to tune every single instrument. Try it!"

As soon as I put the tuning fork on the piano, I feel a tremor run through my body from my fingers to the back of my neck, like once when I wanted to take a lightbulb out of Mamma's bedside table lamp and got an electric shock. She said, "It serves you right. If you'd broken it, I would've smashed the whole lamp over your head." But this is a nice shock; of happiness.

It's time for our snack, but I'm not in the least hungry. Alcide pours himself a glass of red wine. We sit at a little table and eat facing each other like two men. He tells me he didn't learn his craft from his father. He did it all on his own. His father worked the land, but he loves growing things and he loves music, too. He has a musical ear. I don't know what my father did, but I decide there and then that I want to make music when I grow up.

People bring Alcide instruments from all over, even from out of town, and they leave them with him. He sits at his worktable and slowly makes them new again. I love being at the workshop with him. I feel like I'm an instrument myself that needs tuning, and that he'll be able to put me right before I get sent back where I came from.

"Look! This is a guitar, this is a trombone, this is a flute, this is a trumpet, this is a clarinet. Which one do you want to try?"

"Is there a violin?" I ask. "My friend Carolina from the Conservatory plays the violin."

"Playing the violin is really hard," he says. "Sit here."

He gets me set up in front of a piano and shows me how to play the seven notes of the scale that I already know. I try again and again. I start mixing the notes. Just like numbers, the sounds are infinite. I imagine myself as a musician, like the ones I saw in the theater when Carolina and I snuck into the rehearsals. Don Alcide claps. I look up and take a bow. A that very moment, a lady in a fur coat sweeps in.

"Good morning, Mrs. Rinaldi."

"Good morning, Mr. Benvenuti. Has your son come to work with you today? You look so alike."

Alcide and I look a little embarrassed, because it's true we're both redheads.

"You see, you need to start calling me Babbo. Even Mrs. Rinaldi agrees."

As he goes into the storeroom, he adds, "He's not my son. He's staying with us for a while. But for Rosa and I, it's as if he were one of our own kids."

Mrs. Rinaldi and I are left on our own.

"Rosa has family in Sassuolo, if I'm not mistaken. Are you one of them?"

"No, I came on the train. The children's train."

Alcide comes back with the violin and puts it on the counter. I remember Carolina's fingertips made hard by the strings.

"I changed them all," Alcide tells Mrs. Rinaldi.

She sits a pair of glasses on her nose and turns the violin over. She touches all the strings and plucks them to check everything is in order, or to make sure they're not duds. Eventually, she looks satisfied and thanks Alcide. Then she lowers her glasses and looks over them at me, just like she did with her instrument, to make sure I am not a dud.

"They've brought them all the way up here, the poor little things," she says. "But when this little jaunt is over, they'll be going back to their poverty. Wouldn't it have been better to spend all that money helping them back home?"

Alcide puts his hand on my other shoulder and squeezes tight without saying a word.

"I suppose, at the end of the day, this is better than nothing," the lady goes on. "At least you're learning a trade. What do you want to do when you grow up? Tune instruments, too?"

I feel Alcide's hands, which are so light when he repairs instruments, becoming heavy now that he wants to keep me here in this spot and not let me go. I look at the lady, who has taken her violin back, and is about to leave.

"No," I say. "I don't want to tune instruments when I grow up."

Alcide doesn't release one finger from my shoulders, but he leans over to one side to look at me, as if he were seeing me for the first time.

"Ah, no? What then?" the lady says, a little shocked.

"I want to play them. People will pay to listen to me play."

The lady is lost for words and leaves. Finally, I feel a little like Nobèl again, back home on my street.

20

THAT MORNING, ROSA MAKES A CAKE WITH YEL-low custard cream in it, as well as a cheese-and-salami pie. She says she does this for her other kids, too.

Last year, I had a fever. The doctor had to come all the way to the house. Mamma Antonietta's face was white as a sheet, but she didn't cry. Mamma Antonietta never cries. She looked at the photo of my big brother, Luigi, on her bedside table and held her head in her hands. The doctor pulled a face like someone who has left a little *pasta alla genovese* for one last mouthful, and then discovers someone else has eaten it. "You'll need to give him some medicine," he said. Mamma Antonietta waited until he had gone, and then she put her hand into her bra, where she kept the holy card of St. Anthony—the enemy of the devil—and pulled out a hankie with a roll of banknotes inside.

"Last year, I had a nice present," I say, eventually.

Rosa smiles.

"What present would you like this year, now you're with us?"

"Anything is fine," I say. "As long as it's not like last year."

Rosa seals the pie with a thick crust and rubs olive oil onto it with her fingers. The radio is playing some happy music, and she's moving like a dancer I once saw at an American party.

"When Derna gets here, we'll pop it in the oven and eat it nice and warm. Help me lay the table, will you? You're my knight in shining armor today."

She takes my hand and twirls me around the kitchen. Nario watches us from his high chair, clapping his hands, but he is always out of time with the music. Rosa spins around, and I end up stepping on her feet. She laughs, and I go bright red in the face.

"When we were young, Alcide and I would go to the dancing halls. Now I only dance in the kitchen," she said. Mamma and I never danced, even in the kitchen.

Derna comes back early from work. She says there's a surprise for me. I ask her what it is, but she says it will come in its own time. In the meantime, Rosa gets up to fetch the pie and then she goes out to the chicken pen. I follow her to help her, because today I'm her knight. The oven is outside the house, behind the animal pens. I'd never seen it before. I look inside, and it's enormous. It reminds me of the photo Pachiochia showed Mamma to persuade her not to send us on the train. My knees start to wobble, and I bolt and run into the pen. Rosa comes inside and finds me trembling beside the cow that is about to give birth. I'm too scared to look her in the face.

"What's the matter?" she asks. "Is it because of your birthday?"

I shake my head and don't lift my eyes from the ground.

"What's happened? You can tell me, you know. Did someone treat you badly at school? Were they teasing you again?"

I don't say a word. I can feel the cow's warm breath on my neck.

"Have they been giving you trouble? I'll go and talk to them myself."

It had happened in the first few days. Benito Vandelli, one of the boys at the back of the class, called out, "Napoli." He scrunched up his nose every time he came close and said there was a stink of rotten fish. Uliano, the boy who was at the front of the class, but now sits next to me, told me not to take any notice, because everyone had teased Benito the year before, and that was why he was so mean.

That afternoon at the workshop, while we were polishing a piano for a client, Alcide said there was no such thing as bad kids. It was just prejudice. Which is like when you think something before you even think it. Because someone has put it in your head and you can't get it out, however hard you try. He said it was a kind of ignorance and that everyone, not just these kids, needs to watch out and not be prejudiced.

The next day, when Benito called me "Napoli," Uliano told him to shut up and said, "Benito is a Fascist name." Benito didn't answer and went back to his desk in the back row. I thought it wasn't his fault they had given him the wrong name. I realized it was true that even good people have prejudices. Like me, right now. I saw Rosa's enormous oven in the garden and I remembered Pachiochia saying Communists put children in the oven and eat them, and so I ran away and hid in the cattle pen behind the cow that was about to have a calf, and now I've gotten my shoes dirty with cow shit on the day of my birthday party.

"I'm sorry, Rosa. I'm all mixed up. Nobody's ever organized a birthday party for me before, and I've never had a present, except an old tin box Mamma Antonietta gave me. I'm not used to being happy."

Rosa hugs me. Her hands smell of flour and water pastry. I feel the cow's warm breath behind me and Rosa's warm bosom in front of me as she pulls me toward her. Her hair, like Derna's, is as soft as cotton wool, but brown, like her eyes. I don't know why but suddenly I blurt out a confession.

"I'm the mortadella thief."

Rosa strokes my forehead and wipes my eyes with her hand as if she were brushing away my tears.

"We don't have any thieves in this house," she says, taking my hand and leading me back home.

21

A LCIDE COMES IN THE DOOR WITH RIVO AND Luzio. He's singing happily at the top of his voice, *"Libiamo, libiamo nei lieti caliciiiiii . . ."* Let's drink, let's drink from the joyful cups… He holds a package wrapped in colored paper with a ribbon tied in a bow.

"Happy birthday, son! Many happy returns!" he says, and everyone claps except Luzio.

I stand there like a stockfish. They start shouting at me to open the present, but I don't want to rip the paper. I'm hoping it's the wooden rifle I'd seen at the toy store. I untie the ribbon slowly, pull the paper off gently, and find a violin inside. A real violin.

"I made this with my own hands, especially for you" Alcide says. "It's a half-size. I worked on it every evening since the day Mrs. Rinaldi came."

"But I don't know how to play."

"There's a client of mine who teaches music at the Conservatory up in Pesaro. She said she would give you a few lessons to get you started. What is it you always say? 'Nobody's born knowing everything'!"

Alcide chuckles under his mustache.

Rivo comes up and takes the violin out of my hands. He starts screeching the bow across the strings, making a terrible din.

"No, it's not a toy," Alcide says. "You need to treat it with great care. It's your violin and you must always keep it with you. It's yours."

Inside the case, in fact, there's a label with Amerigo Speranza written on it. I am awestruck. I've never had anything of my own before.

"I got a bike for my birthday," Luzio says, staring out the window. "I don't let anyone touch it. It's mine."

I stroke the smooth wood of the instrument and push down on the tightly stretched strings. I run my fingers along the horsehair of the bow.

"Are you happy, son?"

I'm so happy I can't speak.

"Yes, Babbo," I finally manage to say. Alcide opens his arms wide and pulls me into a hug. He smells of aftershave and a little of the glue he uses in the workshop. It's the first time I've been hugged by a father.

"When are we having the cake?" Rivo asks, tugging on Alcide's arm.

"Amerigo doesn't like cake; he only likes mortadella," Luzio says, pointing up at the ceiling. Rosa glares at him, and he shuts up.

"First, there's another surprise," Derna says, pulling a light yellow envelope out of her pocket.

"It's for you, from your mother."

So, Mamma didn't forget my birthday!"

Since I've been up north, we've written three letters to her, but we've never heard back. Derna opens the envelope, sits in an armchair, and I hear Mamma Antonietta's words pouring out of her mouth. I'm plunged back into my life back home. I'm not sure that I like it.

She says she asked Maddalena Criscuolo as a favor to write this letter and to read my letters that have arrived. She says she didn't answer immediately because she was too busy. She says life in our street is the same as ever. The winter has been cold this year, and luckily, I'm up in northern Italy where they keep me warm, dressed, and well fed. She says Zandragliona sends her love and tells me my treasures are safe where we left them. She says Pachiochia has never asked after me but that one can see she's full of bile because all the mothers who sent their kids up north tell everyone how well they are doing, and are slowly turning Communist out of gratitude. She says Capa 'e Fierro is out of jail thanks to his connections, but that he doesn't work with her anymore and has given up his stall at the market.

Derna and I had sent a letter inviting her to come visit at Christmas. She says she can't. That for now, as things stand, it's not possible. She says that anyway the months will go by in no time, and that, before we know it, I'll be back home getting under her feet as usual. She says I was born eight years ago, more or less in this period, and that she hopes her letter gets there in time for my birthday. She says it was cold that day, she felt the pains coming and called the midwife. But by the time she got there, I had already arrived. I had done everything on my own, as usual, and I couldn't wait to get my head out of the sack. I realize she's never told me this before and think that Mamma Antonietta talks more in letters than she does in person.

At the end of the letter, after Maddalena's greetings, there's a crooked scribble. It's her name: Mamma Antonietta. She says Maddalena is teaching her to write her name, at least, so she can put her signature on things when she needs to, instead of a cross. I can picture her, sweating, huffing and puffing, invoking Our Lady of the Arch with every stroke of the pen as she stoops over the brown table, and I'm happy there's a sign that she has made with her own hand, especially for me. Like Alcide's violin.

I ask Derna if we can answer right away, or I'll forget what I want to say. She goes to get some letter paper and a pen and sits at the kitchen table. I dictate, like the teacher does with us at school, and she writes.

I tell Mamma that today is actually my birthday, and that her letter was the best present ever. I don't tell her about the violin, or she may get upset. I tell her that Rosa has made me lots of good things to eat, but that she is still the queen of *alla genovese*. I tell her that I've made a name for myself up in northern Italy, and everyone knows me: the vegetable man, who they call a greengrocer here; the meat man they call a butcher; and the sewing store they call a haberdashery. I tell her there are some trades back home that don't even exist up here, like the water cooler man and the tripe man. In fact, when I asked Derna where I could buy *'o pere e 'o muss*, a delicacy back home I love, her face screwed up into a question mark. She said, "Can you repeat that?" and so I did, but she still didn't understand. I tried again but it was useless. She said she thought I was saying *operemus*, which she said was a word in Latin. "What's Latin?" I asked, and she said it was an ancient language. I said that was possible because *'o pere e 'o muss* is an ancient tradition that consists of eating pig's feet and a calf's head boiled together in a big pot. She finally understood, and we went to the meat man they call the butcher, and he said he had tripe all right but that people up here don't think the feet or heads are special like we do. I sign my name at the bottom of the letter, a little crooked so as not to show her up, and Derna sends greetings, too.

I hope my letter gets there before Holy Night. Last year, it was just the two of us, but at midnight we went out into the street to wish everyone Merry Christmas. Even Capa 'e Fierro came with his wife. She clung to her new bag as if her life depended on it, and looked at Mamma as though she'd stolen something from her.

Everything is different up here. There's no nativity scene. They have a Christmas tree, which has nothing to do with Mary, Joseph, and the baby in the manger. They have a tree. A real tree, with festival lights strung around it and colored balls hanging from its branches like the sausages hanging from their kitchen beams. They say that Father Christmas comes and leaves presents under it. Well, he's never come to my house. Maybe because he couldn't find a Christmas tree there. The kids here say he must've come, because he goes to all children. They say he dresses in red and has a long white beard. That's when I thought maybe he only goes to visit the Communist kids. The only person who ever brought us anything was Capa 'e Fierro, but he doesn't have a beard, white or black, and he doesn't dress in red. Capa 'e Fierro has brown hair and blue eyes, and I would never call him Father, not even at Christmas.

Derna folds the letter in four and puts it in the envelope. But I tell Derna I want to send a present to Mamma Antonietta, so she can put it under a tree, like they do here. There's a tree right outside Zandragliona's tenement apartment: a lemon tree. Derna says I can draw a picture and we can put it in the envelope with the letter. I've never drawn a picture in my life.

"It's easy," she says. "I'll help you."

She sits me on her knee, takes my hand in hers, and we start moving the pencil together. We draw faces, hands, noses, and eyes. Then we draw hair and clothes. Rivo goes to get his pencil case because Derna says the picture will be nicer with lots of colors, and we fill the page with pink, yellow, and blue. Derna's silky hair tickles my neck while our hands move up and down the page until the faces appear on it.

Mamma Antonietta appears in her good dress with little flowers. I've drawn her at Zandragliona's house on Christmas Eve, with Maddalena Criscuolo and Capa 'e Fierro, without his wife. In Zandragliona's tenement apartment I've drawn Ciccio Cheese, who may be back home waiting for me, and the monkey trained by the old man. It looks just like the cave in Bethlehem. At least in my drawing, I think, she'll be in good company over Christmas.

22

U LIANO HASN'T COME TO SCHOOL, BECAUSE HE
has a fever. I ask my teacher whether by any chance it's
bronchial asthma, like my brother Luigi's, but he says it's mumps.
That's lucky, otherwise I'd be left all alone again. Luzio's always in
the front row, and Benito is sitting next to me. We're getting along
fine now; he doesn't pinch his nose anymore when he sees me, and
I let him copy the math problems sometimes.

During recess, everyone gets up and gathers into little gangs,
but Benito and I sit in our places, and we each do our own thing.
Mr. Ferrari stands behind his desk watching me.

"Speranza, Benvenuti, come up to my desk."

Luzio and I look at each other for the first time since the mortadella fiasco.

"Speranza," he says, "a new girl has arrived on a train from the
same city as you. The principal wants us to give the girl a nice
welcome and make her feel right at home."

I look at Benito and hope the new girl doesn't get the same welcome I did.

Outside the principal's office, Rivo is waiting for me, together with the fifth-grade teacher. He tells me the new girl's going to be in his class, because they're the same age, and she'd already been to school. The principal calls us in.

"Please!" he says, and we go in. He is tall and bald and looks just like the man in the photograph in Alcide and Rosa's house. I ask my teacher if by any chance the principal's name is Lenin, like the man who taught everyone about communism. He looks at the principal as if he were seeing him for the first time and bursts out laughing. The principal stands up, walks out from behind his desk, and introduces us to the new girl. He says her name is Rossana, and that she is the daughter of an important comrade. She was supposed to stay with the Manzi family, but Signora Manzi is in bed with pneumonia, so Rossana and her governess, Signorina Adinolfi, are going to be looked after by the priest until Signora Manzi gets better.

Rossana is taller than me. She has green eyes, long black braids, and an angry scowl on her face. Maybe because, instead of a family, she ended up with Signorina Adinolfi at the priest's house.

"This is Amerigo," my teacher says, giving me a little shove forward. "He's been here with us for more than a month and he's getting on very well. These are his new brothers." Rivo smiles, revealing the gap between his front teeth. Luzio tuts when he hears the word *brothers*, but then goes red when he looks at the girl. She doesn't look at me and she doesn't say thank you or goodbye.

On our way home that afternoon, Luzio hangs back and walks alongside his brother, rather than striding ahead on his own as usual, and peppers him with questions about the new girl with the braids.

"My teacher says she's going to Derna's for supper tonight," Rivo says. "The mayor is coming, too. He wants to meet her and Amerigo."

"What about us? That's not fair!" Luzio says.

"We were born here, stupid. We didn't come here on a train."

"So what? Just because we were born here, he doesn't want to meet us?"

Rivo looks puzzled but then he smiles, the gap in his teeth showing.

"Maybe we can go, too, and meet the mayor?" he says.

"Of course. We can't leave him on his own, can we?"

SIGNORINA ADINOLFI ACCOMPANIES ROSSANA TO the house, but has to leave immediately to prepare the priest's evening meal. The girl sits at the kitchen table and looks down at the floor. She's wearing a different dress from the one she had on this morning. This one is red, with black velvet trimmings. I run to my room and switch the light on and off three times. On the other side of the road, I can see the light going on and off three times in Rivo's window. This is the signal Rivo taught me. When I go back into the kitchen, the girl is as still as a statue.

"Do you want to play a little before dinner?" Derna asks her.

She doesn't answer. Maybe she's scared they'll cut her tongue off, like Mariuccia before she found her new blond mother. There's a knock at the door. Derna goes to open it, and we find ourselves alone.

"Look, Pachiochia was telling lies," I say, sticking my tongue out.

She doesn't know what I'm talking about. She thinks I'm teasing her by making a stupid face.

"Come in, Alfeo," Derna says. "The kids are in the kitchen."

The mayor is carrying two colorfully wrapped gifts. One for me, and one for Rossana.

"I'm here to welcome you on behalf of this town," he says, handing us the packages. The girl doesn't move a muscle. She's not even interested in the present. I take mine, but I don't open it, because I want to wait until Rivo and Luzio get here.

Rivo and I play on the floor with the toy train Mayor Alfeo gave me, while Luzio sits as still as he can next to the girl. It looks like he's caught the same disease.

When the tortellini are dished up, everyone starts slurping them into their mouths, except the girl. The mayor looks happy.

"I didn't know you were a good cook as well as everything else," he says to Derna.

"My mother made the tortellini," Luzio boasts.

"Derna can cook, too," I say. "And she's good at being a union leader."

"I'm not good at anything; that's why they made me mayor," the mayor says, laughing.

"Don't believe a word of what he says, kids. Alfeo was a brave partisan during the war. He was sent to jail and even exiled."

"What does *exiled* mean?" I ask.

"It means I was sent for a long time far away from home, from my town, from the people I love, and I wasn't allowed to come back."

"Don't you get it? Exiled. Like you and me." It was Rossana's voice speaking. Nobody had ever heard it.

"You're not exiled," the mayor said. "You're among friends who want to help you. Rather, you're among comrades, who are better than friends, because friendship is a private matter between two people, and it can come to an end. Comrades, on the other hand, fight together, because they believe in the same ideals."

"My father is a comrade of yours. I'm not. I don't need your charity, and I don't want it."

Derna puts her spoon down and makes the face she usually makes when she comes back from a union meeting that has gone badly. The mayor raises his hand to signal that he will answer.

"You can't have tasted these tortellini. They taste of hospitality, not of charity," he says, smiling. "Isn't that right?" he says, looking at me. I nod, but I'm not so sure anymore. Rossana's words have confused me. This evening, Rosa's tortellini don't taste as good as usual; they taste a little bit of charity, and I'm scared I won't be able to overcome the nasty taste in my mouth.

"My parents should have given me hospitality at home, not the strangers here."

Rossana speaks like an adult who says what she thinks. When I hear her say these things, I feel as though I believe them myself. Derna starts clearing the table and gives us kids permission to get down. Rivo and I go back to the train set, and the mayor unwraps the present he brought for Rossana. Inside, there's a felt puppet in the shape of a dog, with big sad eyes. The mayor puts his hand inside and starts making funny sounds. The dog leaps, turns somersaults, wags its tail, and finally curls up on Rossana's lap. She lifts her hand and rests it on the dog's head. She doesn't say a word, but a tear is slowly trickling down her cheek. Luzio, who has been sitting like a statue next to Rossana, takes a hankie out of his pocket and presses it into her hand. She picks it up and wipes the tear away.

23

A FEW DAYS LATER, WHILE WE'RE DOING ADDI-
tion in columns, I see Rivo's teacher running toward Principal Lenin's office through the open door of our classroom. She
is shouting and on the verge of tears.

"She asked to go to the bathroom. Minutes went by, and I asked
her deskmate here to go and see if she was not feeling well. Right,
Ginetta?"

The girl, who had followed her teacher to the principal's office,
nods, her blond curls tumbling over her head. Snot is dripping
out of her nose and mixing with her tears. Then the principal,
the teachers, and the janitors start hunting for the new girl all
over the school: the classrooms, the secretaries' office, the storeroom, the library. There is no sign of her. Rossana has vanished.

"How come nobody saw her leave the school?" the principal
shouts, red in the face. His eyes are like the devil's, which makes
him look even more like the man in the photograph at Rosa's

house. The custodian had gone to the bathroom himself, it turns out. The new girl had taken the opportunity to slip out.

"Should we call the parents?" Mr. Ferrari asks the principal.

The principal looks around him as if he were lost.

"No," he says finally, looking down at the floor. "Let's not make this public yet. I'll take responsibility. It's a small town, and how far could a little girl have gone on foot, after all? We'll find her, you'll see. Let's wait until this evening, and then if we don't find her . . ."

In the streets, nobody talks about anything but the little girl who ran away from school. Mr. Ferrari told us not to worry, that the adults will take care of it.

"Adults always decide everything," Luzio says as we are walking home. "What we want doesn't count for a thing. You, too. You didn't want to come here. They forced you, right?"

I don't know whether Mamma forced me or not, but I don't say anything. I walk in silence and think about Rossana, about her face that evening she came to supper, her mouth turned downward and her eyes made of stone. Rivo goes to fetch water for the animals, and I follow him. The expecting cow looks sad. Sick, actually. Her mouth is turned downward, too. But she doesn't run away. She stays where she is.

"Derna?" I say before going to sleep. "Is it cold outside?" She understands what I'm getting at right away and takes my hand. She gives it a big squeeze. Maybe they've found her by now. Alfeo is hardheaded; he's not one to give up easily. He was a partisan up in the mountains. There's no way he's going to let a little girl with braids get away.

Derna leaves a glass of water by my bed, as she does every evening, and turns the light off. I close my eyes, but sleep is the last thing that comes to me. There's too much noise, and everything tumbles around in my mind: Rossana's downturned mouth like the sad cow, the felt dog, the partisan mayor, Mr. Ferrari's reassurances, the mortadella hanging from the ceiling, the train trip with all the other kids, the bus where I fell asleep with no shoes on. I finally understand Luzio was right. Adults don't get kids. I look out the window to see whether they're still up. I flash my light three times. No answer. I try again, on and off three times. I go back to bed. Maybe they're already asleep. But then the signal comes: one, two, three. I get dressed quickly, put on my shoes, heavy jacket, and hat, cut off a nice big chunk from the round of parmesan cheese on the sideboard, and slip out of the house as quietly as I can. I cross the road and wait near the chicken pen. There's total silence. All you can hear are the groans of the pregnant cow every now and again. The cold creeps up from the ground into my shoes. I'm tempted to go back inside and wrap myself in my warm covers, but I see a light coming toward me. It's Luzio with a lantern.

"I didn't wake Rivo up," he says. "If I did, he'd tell Mamma."

"I may know where Rossana's gone," I tell him. "Do you know how to get to where the bus stops?"

"Let's go!" he answers.

WE WALK SIDE BY SIDE, HARDLY SAYING A WORD. The roads are empty, but he knows his way and isn't scared. I am, a little. I take my hand out of my pocket and reach out for his. Luzio gives me three soft squeezes, like our secret light signal. We get to the place where the bus stops after walking for half an hour or longer. The last bus for Bologna is pulling out, its engine on, and its headlights beaming toward the ticket office. Together with Luzio, we run in to take a look. There are three men and a woman. Rossana is not there. I've gotten it all wrong, I think. It's late, and the sky is pitch black.

"Let's go back home," Luzio says. "It's cold."

We go into the waiting room to warm up a little and sit on the bench to rest. Finally, we see her. She's sitting in a corner, downcast, her usual serious expression on her face. I signal to Luzio to stay put and not say a word, and I approach her slowly, slowly. I sit next to her, and as soon as she sees me, she jumps up and makes as if she's going to run away. Then she stops. She doesn't know where else to go. I take the lump of cheese that I had brought along out of my coat pocket and offer it to her. She takes it without saying anything and eats it in two mouthfuls. She hasn't eaten a thing since this morning.

"I know everything is strange at the beginning," I say. "I understand you . . ."

"What do you think you understand?" she answers in that grown-up voice of hers. "I'm not like you," she says. "I'm not like any of you."

Her words upset me. I don't understand what she's saying. Luzio is sitting on the bench opposite us, waiting. Rossana tries to fix her braids, which are coming loose.

"We've never lacked for anything back home. Do you know where I live? If I tell you, you'll have a good laugh. One of the most beautiful streets in the city. My father forced me to come, so that we would look good. To give an example to others, he said. My mother begged him, but he wouldn't budge. Why *me* of all people, when I'm the youngest in the family? What's it to do with me? It's not fair! It's just not *fair*!"

She starts sobbing. One braid has come undone, and the red

ribbon has dropped on the floor. The stationmaster notices us and comes over.

"Where are your parents, little ones?"

"Far away," Rossana says, crying her eyes out. "Very far away!"

Luzio and I explain the whole situation, and he says, "I'll call Mayor Corassori right away."

He comes in person. He's as relaxed as he was the other evening at dinner, and smiles when he sees us.

"What a lucky evening this is: three brave kids in one fell swoop! But you made a big mistake," he says, looking at Rossana. "You don't run away like that without first tasting Rosa's tortellini, not to mention the mortadella . . ."

I check on Luzio from the corner of my eye, but he doesn't say anything. Maybe he's not even listening. He bends down, picks up the red ribbon that had fallen out of Rossana's hair, and puts it in his pocket.

When we knock on the door, there's no answer, and all the lights are out. Then we hear a terrible roar coming from the cow pen. We rush in and see Rosa with her hands covered in blood. Rossana screams and runs out. I hide behind the mayor, while Luzio runs up to his mother. A minute later, we hear another, softer moan, like a baby crying. Rosa beckons us in, and even Rossana comes back to take a look. The cow is lying there sweating, looking like she's just seen death. The newborn calf's eyes are still sticky, and it groans with hunger. Rossana approaches it, her hands shaking. As soon as she sees it, though, she smiles and reaches out to stroke its muzzle.

"Eat, little one. Your mother is right here beside you."

It smells its mother and starts suckling. Rivo appears from the back of the pen carrying some fresh hay.

"Since you were wandering around at night without me, I'll choose the new calf's name," he says, smiling.

"Not fair," Luzio says. "It's my turn to choose the name."

"Luzio's right," Rosa says. "It is his turn, even though you still need to explain why you're here with the mayor at this time of the night."

Luzio looks at the calf, then at me, then at the calf again.

"I've decided; I want to call it Amerigo," he says, walking out of the pen.

I'm struck dumb, and for a moment nothing feels real. The calf has stopped suckling and has curled up under his mother, fast asleep. Its legs are like twigs, and its fur is matted. It's so thin that when it breathes, you can count its ribs. And it has the same name as me.

When we are all sitting in the kitchen, Rosa wants to know why we went out on our own in the dark.

"They went out to find a certain something that was lost. It was heroic, Rosa. Don't tell them off. They deserve a medal."

I try to picture Mamma's face when I get home with a medal, like Maddalena Criscuolo.

THE NEXT DAY AT SCHOOL, PRINCIPAL LENIN CALLS me and Luzio into his office and pins a medal and a red, green, and white rosette on our chests. Our classmates crowd around, asking us how things went, and when we tell the story, we make it seem much more adventurous than it actually was. Rossana comes to say goodbye during the break. Her hair is tightly braided again, and she's wearing a nice light blue dress. She beams us a smile for the first time, as she tells us her father's coming to get her and take her home. Luzio pulls the red ribbon out of his pocket and hands it to her.

"You keep it," Rossana says. "To remember me by."

Luzio closes his fist, and the ribbon disappears into his hand.

Mr. Ferrari tells us all to go back to our places and, since Benito has gotten mumps, too, everyone wants to sit next to me.

"It's my place," Luzio says. "I'm his brother."

And he comes to sit at the back of the class with me.

24

THE CHRISTMAS VACATION HAS STARTED. WE never saw Rossana again. On New Year's Day, we went to see the band playing in the town hall, and the mayor told us her father had come a few days before Christmas to pick her up. Rossana was right. She's not like me at all. She had left a greeting card for the three of us, but Luzio hadn't wanted even to read it. Bad luck, I think. She's missing the Epiphany Partisan Festival that Derna has organized.

The big square with the tall, tall bell tower is crisscrossed with strings of lights and bunting. The Communist ladies are dressed up as Befana witches with torn shoes and big noses. Rivo and Luzio laugh. I don't, because I used to have shoes with holes in them. They hurt, and there's nothing to laugh about. The witches hand out bags of candy and a wooden puppet to all the kids, whether they were from the north or from the south. Alcide and Rosa are drinking red wine and dancing, while Rivo, Luzio, and I play with our school friends. Nario is lying in his stroller sleeping, even though there is music playing and people shouting, because he's already eaten. When the games begin, we three brothers are put on the same team, and we win a rosette and an orange. I've never won anything before, not even the raffle Pachiochia used to organize on the last day of the year, because Mamma didn't have the money to buy a ticket.

When they line us up to form a choir, I find myself right next to a kid with jet-black curls combed back with gel. I almost don't recognize him.

"Amerì, is that you? You look like a movie star!"

"Stop teasing, Tommasì. How much salami have you eaten? You're as fat as Pachiochia."

On the other side of the piazza I spot the man with the mustache, who had picked him out, and his wife, who has muscled arms and big breasts. There were two older brothers there, too, who also had mustaches and looked just like their father. Tommasino's babbo waved at him as we were singing, and for a moment I thought Tommasino was beginning to look like his new father, too.

Luzio is two rows in front of me in the choir, and he turns around and looks back every now and again out of curiosity. Usually he's the one who knows everyone, and I don't know a living soul. But now it's the opposite. I see the short boy with black hair, the blond one with gaps in his mouth, whose teeth have now grown in, and lots of other kids who were on the train with me. Except that now they are all well dressed and healthy-looking, and it's hard to tell who comes from down south and who was born up north.

Tommasino and I reckon Mariuccia must be in the crowd, too, so we go off to look for her. We're looking for a thin little blond girl with hair as short as a hatchling's, but she isn't there. After a while, we sit on a bench near the sandwich bar. We ask a partisan Befana witch to pour us some orange juice and watch the other kids playing tag. Luzio comes and sits with us, and after a while, Tommasino starts telling him about us painting the sewer rats. But luckily, at that very moment, Mariuccia suddenly appears. She's walking between the parents who had picked her out on our first day here, holding their hands on each side. Her hair has grown into long blond curls like an actress in a movie poster. Her face is round, and her dress is dark pink, like her cheeks. She has a waistband made of woven flowers and a garland of the same flowers in her hair. Mariuccia has turned beautiful!

When Tommaso and I see her, we're paralyzed. Neither of us is brave enough to call her name or show our faces, but as soon as she recognizes us, she hugs us really tight. It's just Mariuccia, but it feels different somehow; to Tommasino, too. I can see.

"How's it going?" Mariuccia asks, in a strong local accent.

"*Màma, Babbo,*" she says to the blond lady and her husband. "These are my pals from down south." That's when I understand that Mariuccia will never be going home, because she's found her family here.

Before going back home myself, I want to finish up all the things I still need to do here. I have to build a secret hideout behind the animal pen with Rivo and Luzio. I have to train the new calf that they called Amerigo in my honor. I have to learn to play the violin with Maestro Serafini. When I first started, I was convinced it was not going to be my strong point. My fingers hurt, and instead of making music, I sounded like a cat in heat. From Alcide's workshop windows, I would watch the other kids throwing snowballs, while I spent hours and hours with my violin teacher, practicing my scales. Then, one evening, after all that practice, the violin stopped screeching and meowing, and I finally heard music. I couldn't believe I had produced it with my own hands.

Another thing I need to do is help Derna organize communism, because she gets tired doing it all alone. She works a lot; after a day's work, in the evening she picks me up at Rosa's house. Then she sits in bed with me, we talk about our day, and she reads me a story about animals, who are always either good or bad. There's a fox, a wolf, a frog, and a crow. Every two or three pages, there's a color picture. Every now and again, Derna puts her finger under the words and says, "You read now." Or if we're really tired out, she sings me a song to send me to sleep. Since we realized she didn't know any lullabies at all, she sings other songs that she does know, like "Bandiera Rossa," which is about a red flag that triumphs and brings freedom. When it comes to the last line, I change the words from *"Evviva il comunismo e la libertà"* to *"Evviva Derna, Rosa e la li-ber-tà!"*

When she was organizing the Epiphany Partisan Festival, she asked my advice on how to decorate the stockings, what games to play, and which songs to make the orchestra play. One evening, though, after the final meeting to organize the festival, Derna came to get me at Rosa's with a dark expression on her face. Rivo, Luzio, and I were playing with the wooden building blocks Alcide had made for us. Usually, Derna would stop awhile in the kitchen and drink a glass of red wine while we went on playing and shouting that we didn't want to stop just yet. But that evening, she didn't even take her coat off, and she took me home immediately. Derna didn't say a word. I thought it was my fault. I must have given her some wrong advice, and now she was angry with me. When she took her hat off, I saw her cheek was bright red, as if she'd had too much sun or gotten too cold. When we sat down at the kitchen table, she burst into tears. I'd never seen her cry before, so I started crying, too. Mamma Antonietta never cries, either. For as long as I've known her, at least. We sat there, like two idiots, at the kitchen table, weeping into our bowls of pasta in broth. She didn't want to tell me what was wrong. She said it was nothing. We went to bed, with no animal stories, or songs, or anything.

The next day was Saturday. While I was playing hide-and-seek with Luzio, I heard Derna talking to Rosa. I heard her say that a big-shot comrade had come to the meeting. He had no complaints at all about the organization of the festival, because she and the others had done a good job. Then the big shot had asked to speak to her on her own. She had explained to him everything she'd done for the union and the election campaign, and he'd told her that she'd be better off concentrating on children's parties and charity for the poor. I had found a hiding place in the kitchen, wedged between the wood stove and the larder, so that I could listen to them. Derna had told the big shot that there were plenty of women who had fought alongside the partisans, who had used rifles, and had won medals. I remembered Maddalena Criscuolo's medal and her saving the Sanità bridge from being blown up. The big shot had asked her if she wanted a medal, too. Derna had answered that many women deserved a medal just for sticking with the Party. That was when he had given her a hard slap on the cheek. She hadn't cried, she told Rosa. I stayed down in my hiding place. I didn't know what to say. Mamma Antonietta would never have taken a slap without striking back. She would have given the comrade at least two slaps back. But Derna hadn't done anything. She'd just started singing the song about women not being scared if they're in a union: *sebben che siamo donne, paura non abbiamo* . . . Since it was one of the lullabies that she often sang to me before going to sleep, I decided to come out of my hiding

25

CHRISTMAS HAD PASSED, AND SO HAD EPIPH-
any. The apple Mamma gave me when I left has been on my
desk all this time. I wanted to keep it to remember her by but, day
after day, it has dried up and gone brown. It's inedible now.

"Rosa," I say one day after school. "When will I be leaving?"

Rosa stops shelling the beans and sits there in silence, looking
pensive.

"Why? Don't you like it here? Do you miss your mamma?"

"No, yes, well, just a little . . ." I say. "It's just that I'm scared that
if too much time goes by, I won't miss her anymore."

Rosa gives me a handful of beans to shell.

"Can you see how many beans there are in each pod? There's
room for lots of them. Like in your heart."

She opens one and shows me.

"Count them!" she says.

I run my fingers over each bean.

"Seven," I say.

"You see?" she says. "That's all of us: Alcide and me, Derna, the kids, and your mother. You can keep us all together."

I like helping her with the beans, splitting the tough pods with my thumbs and popping the moist white seeds out. I like the sound of the beans as they ping into the earthenware casserole dish, and the sight of the speckled shells piling up higher and higher on the kitchen table.

Rosa turns her head and gazes through the window.

"It will be time to leave when the fields have turned yellow, and the wheat has grown high."

I give a quick glance to see how high the wheat has grown, but there's no sign yet. The air is cold, and the countryside gray.

A week later, the weather turns warm. One evening, Derna comes to get me after work and says, "Tomorrow we're all going to Bologna on the bus."

I run to the window to check the fields, but the wheat isn't high yet.

"Are you sending me away already?" I ask. Our secret hideout isn't finished yet.

"When he plays the violin, we need to put plugs in our ears," Luzio teases.

I'd like to answer that this isn't true anymore, because my violin teacher says I'm learning fast and that I have great talent, but then I realize he's probably just saying it so I don't get sent home.

Derna says it isn't time yet. We're going to Bologna because there's a surprise.

The next day, we all jump off the bus, dressed in our Sunday best. We walk to the building where we were first entrusted to our new families. When we get there, all the tables are laid like that day, and the band is playing. I cling to Derna for fear they'll take me away, because everything looks exactly the same as that day, like a journey back through time.

When the band starts playing, Derna climbs up onto the wooden stage and I'm left alone again. I want to tell her to come down and not to sing, because I've never told her, but she sings a little out of tune. Luckily, she only has to speak. She says we have an important guest, an intelligent woman who doesn't have any prejudices and who has come in person to see how the children who came up on the trains are doing. She says this woman has just endured a long and tiring journey to take news back to our mothers. There is a roll of drums from the band, and a short, squat woman with her hair pulled up in a bun and a red, white, and green sash across her breast joins Derna on the stage.

I'm stunned. I can see Tommasino in the front row with his new mustached babbo. I push through the crowd and say, "Let's run: Pachiochia has found us!"

He can't hear me because, in the meantime, Pachiochia has picked up the microphone and started to shout into it. She says how happy she is to be here in person. She says that, to tell the truth, she harbored some doubts about the train transports to begin with, but now she is here and she can see how well fed and well dressed we are, she feels a little bit Communist herself, even though she is devoted to our king and will always be a monarchist. She smiles her toothless smile, and people start cheering. Pachiochia bows her head a little, like a singer at the Piedigrotta Festival.

Derna has gotten down from the stage and comes to stand next to me and Tommasino.

"How did she find us?" I ask.

"We invited her," Derna said. "To prove to everybody that you still have all your hands and feet in the right place, and that none of you have been taken to Russia."

"So she's not going to take us back then?" I ask, just to make sure.

Tommasino turns to me, pokes me with his elbow, and sticks a horizontal finger over his upper lip.

"Pachiochia did the right thing to come here," he says. "Everyone up north has a mustache."

Pachiochia is taken around the room, and the mayor offers her little tastes of all the gastronomic specialties of the area. She eats, drinks, and talks constantly. I see her going up to every kid, asking which quarter they are from back home, who their mother is, who their father is, how they are, if they are doing well in school, and so on. All the kids say practically the same thing: that is, at the beginning they missed home, but now they have gotten used to it and are better off than they were. Tommasino and I go up to her and tug at her dress.

"Donna Pachiochia, Donna Pachiochia," we chant in chorus. She doesn't recognize us at first. Then, when she does, she bares her gums at us.

"Have you noticed? Here there is dig-ni-ty!"

She tries to give me a hug.

"Come here, my beautiful boy," she said. "Goodness me, how you've grown. Antonietta will hardly recognize you when you come home. Come here, give me a kiss."

She bends down and I feel her whiskery lips on my face. Tommasino manages to get away. I ask her about Mamma Antonietta and Zandragliona and about life on our street. She had made such a big fuss when we were getting on the trains, and now, when I get home, I wonder whether instead of the photograph of the mustached king on her bedroom wall, I would find a picture of the bald man who looks just like the principal of my school.

At the end of the party, they take a picture of us all.

"Smile!" the photographer shouts as he's about to snap. But Pachiochia isn't satisfied.

"Wait!"

She turns to us and asks us all to raise both hands.

"This photograph will be proof for the tongue waggers that your hands have not been cut off!"

When I see the picture in the school hall, it is living proof: our teeth bared in a cheesy smile and our fingers waving in the air.

26

DERNA PROMISED WE WOULD GO ON THE FIRST really sunny day of the season. And the day has arrived today. We woke up late because it was Sunday. I opened my eyes and I saw a white light coming through the shutters and shining in stripes across my sheets. When I looked out the window, I saw that the fields were turning yellow, and the wheat was growing, though it wasn't too high yet.

I went into the kitchen and saw that Derna was all ready to go. She was wearing a lovely light-colored dress I'd never seen before. When she goes to work, she always wears a white blouse and a gray skirt and jacket. She used to wear a black suit, but then she said she was no longer in mourning, and that life had to go on. I saw him once in a photo Derna keeps hidden in her bag. She takes it with her everywhere and never lets anyone look at it. But once she showed it to me. She said he had been really brave; a real comrade. She said he had been killed in an attack against the Fascists. Then she closed her bag and said nothing else. Today, though, she has put all her dark clothes away, and she's wearing the light-colored dress.

The man in the photo was thin, with a happy face. Rosa said I looked like him. She said he had light hair and blue eyes, like me. Derna had met him at a Party conference. She had been giving a speech surrounded by men, with Rosa and Alcide sitting in the audience listening. At one point, a group of young men had come in and stood near the window. Derna had looked around and caught sight of him for the first time. She had blushed bright red and almost lost her train of thought. But then she had recovered and managed to get to the end of her speech.

The young man had fallen in love with her and wanted to marry her after the war. But he was two years younger than her, and the Party bosses didn't want them to get married. Rosa says the Party bosses can be worse than village gossips. They fill their mouths with talk of freedom, but then they don't allow their members to be free. Especially the women. Derna suffered the consequences.

After the tragedy, she dressed only in black and never spoke to anyone about him ever again. She threw herself into her work and stifled her smiles. "And then you came along," Rosa had said, combing my hair with her hands like she did with her own boys.

Derna pulls her dress down over her hips. She looks younger today. She's even put a touch of lipstick on.

"Today we're all going to the beach," she says, filling a basket with cheese and salted pork sandwiches and a bottle of water. She has set some new clothes out for me to wear: a white short-sleeved shirt, a pair of blue shorts, ankle socks, and a pair of T-bar sandals. I've stopped counting points for the shoes, because everyone here has either new shoes or hardly worn ones, so there's no fun in the game anymore. And anyhow, even if I did get to a hundred, what would I ask for since I already have everything I need?

I feel like running. I start running around the kitchen, around the table, three times, four times, and I end up falling into Derna's arms. I cling to her as tightly as I can with both arms. She wobbles and loses her balance, and we both roll onto the sofa. But I don't let go of her. I hold on tight, my face sinking into her belly, and I smell her flesh. Derna is hugging me tight, and she doesn't let go of me, either. We lie there on the sofa in our spring outfits, in each other's arms like a couple of newlyweds.

When Alcide knocks on the door with Rivo and Luzio, Derna picks up the basket and sets off with Rosa, who is carrying the little one in her arms. We walk toward the bus that will take us to the beach. On the short walk, we all sing the song about freedom at the top of our voices, the one I changed the words to: "Long live Derna, Rosa, and freedom."

By the time we get to the beach, the sun is high, and the air is hot. The sea is calm and smooth as if it's been combed flat. There are lots of kids already there. Many of them were on the train with me. As soon as Tommasino sees me, he starts throwing sand balls at me.

Mariuccia is nowhere to be seen. Tommasino says the couple who picked her out would like to keep her forever.

"What about her cobbler father?" I ask.

Tommasino rolls his pants up and takes his socks off. He looks at me, rolls his eyes, and says the cobbler father will see it as a favor if they take the girl off his hands. I look at Derna, Rosa, and Alcide. Who knows? Might they want to keep me forever, too?

"My babbo here says I can come back whenever I want; the door is always open. He says they'll take their summer vacation down south and carry on taking care of me. Even from far away, they'll still be helping me."

I take my shorts off and stay in the blue-and-white-striped swimsuit Derna has given me. Tommasino takes one look and bursts out laughing.

"What are you doing? Are you going to stand there in front of everyone in your underpants?"

"It's a bathing costume."

"I thought you said the sea had no purpose?"

"Wanna bet?"

I race across the beach and start paddling in the sea. The sand under my feet is cold and sticky. I feel my toes sinking down into the wet sand, but I keep walking until the water is up to my knees. It's cold, but I don't want to give Tommasino the satisfaction. I want him to see that I'm like one of the kids from up north.

Derna used to be a good swimmer, and she has shown me what to do. I'm confident I'll do just fine. Tommasino calls to me from the beach.

"Amerì, where are you going?"

I turn to look at him, but keep on going. I see Derna talking to some other ladies, sitting under a beach umbrella.

"Derna, look at me!" I shout.

As soon as she turns to look at me, I dive in. The freezing cold water covers my face and my head. I kick my legs and paddle with my arms as fast as I can, as Derna has explained, and manage to pull my head up out of the water. But then I taste the salty flavor of the sea as it fills my mouth and blocks my nose and I can't breathe. I go back underwater, and I can't open my eyes.

I didn't think seawater was like this. It looks light but then, when it covers your head, it's really heavy, and it pushes you down to the bottom. As I sink further under, I remember Derna's words and paddle even more desperately with my hands and feet, but they have gone weak. I barely manage to get my head out of the water, and open my eyes. I see Tommasino yelling, his hair wild and curly like it was before his babbo here greased his hair back. I see Derna running barefoot along the beach, her pretty dress hitched up around her legs. I can't see her face, because I can't touch the ground and because the water is starting to cover my eyes again. But I'm pretty sure it's the same face she made that day after the meeting with the big shot. I'm sinking. I squeeze my eyes shut and feel the salt burning my throat. I can't breathe.

All of a sudden, I feel strong hands grabbing my wrists. They're Derna's hands. I feel her holding on to me and not letting me go, fighting against the water. The weight on my head feels less heavy, like the layers of darkness covering my eyes, and Derna's arms, which are stronger than the force of the sea, bring me up to the surface again. Then I see black. Mamma Antonietta's face and Zandragliona's laugh, and then nothing.

When I open my eyes, Derna's hands are pressing down on my chest and, with every thrust, more salt water spouts out of my mouth and nose. Rosa wraps me up in a blanket she had brought to the beach for us to lie on, while Alcide sticks a bottle of vinegar under my nose. Rivo, Luzio, and all the other kids are standing around in stony silence. Tommasino is still bawling his eyes out and doesn't seem to be calming down.

Derna's hair is wet and her lipstick has been washed off. I can see her eyes right up close. They are as gray as the sea.

"Don't leave me," I say, gripping on to her.

27

THE FIELDS ARE YELLOW, THE WHEAT HAS grown high, but there's no sun today. A light mist covers the street and it feels like we'll never get there.

Rosa has given me a paper bag full of sandwiches for the journey. In my suitcase, she has packed some homemade ravioli to take home, as well as jars of peach, plum, and apricot jam. Before leaving, I helped her pull the cheese-and-salami pie out of the oven behind the house. She wrapped it in greased paper, and then in a yellow-and-white-striped tea cloth.

"This is for you," she said. Then she took the other loaves she had baked for home. They'll be eating them at lunchtime without me.

Rivo and Luzio waited outside the animal pen to go and carve our names into the wooden shelter we had built together. We each wrote our own name and then Rivo grabbed the penknife and engraved in capitals the name BENVENUTI under all three.

"This is our house," he said. It was strange seeing my name linked to their family name but I was happy anyway.

Alcide called out to me.

"Come along, son, or we'll miss the bus."

Rivo and Luzio came to say goodbye.

"Wait here," I said to them, and ran into the house. When I came back, I reached out and handed Luzio the marble he had given me on my first day.

"You keep it," he said. "I know you'll bring it when you come back. You're not a thief, right?" He smiled and wiped his eyes with the sleeve of his jacket.

ON THE BUS, ALCIDE IS QUIET, AND SO IS DERNA. After the episode at the beach, Derna put her light-colored dress away and packed away her smile. For my departure today, she's wearing that same white blouse and gray skirt. It's gray outside, too. In the mist, all you can see are a few trees and dark shadows of houses. The rain splashes off the windows drop by drop, then flows in rivulets.

"Finally, a little rain after all this heat," Alcide says.

He hadn't said a word since we left.

"We need rain for the crops. Sometimes things that feel bad are actually good. Right, Derna? Our Amerigo is going back to his mother. We should be happy for him!"

Derna doesn't answer. I hate it when she's sad. I take my shoes off, like I did on my way here, and whisper in her ear, "Shall we sing the song about the women?"

Derna gives a fake smile and starts singing. The song comes out real, not fake. Softly, to begin with, then, when we get off the bus, louder and louder. It's Maddalena's song about the women not being scared, because they love their children: *"Sebben che siamo donne, paura non abbiamo, per amore dei nostri figli, per amor dei nostri figli . . .*" and when she sings the word *figli*, she squeezes my hand like she did when she pulled me out of the sea. Alcide and I join in, too. The three of us are singing our heads off, in the middle of the street, and in the train station, one on each side of me, holding my hands all the way to the platform, and then up onto the train, without ever stopping.

THE TRAIN IS FULL OF KIDS, BUT THERE ARE FEWER than when we came up. Some have stayed behind with their new northern parents, like Mariuccia, and others have already gone back, because they couldn't deal with being homesick and angry, like Rossana. I see Tommasino in the middle of the crowd, his hair combed back with gel. His babbo's mustache has grown even longer, and he has curled up the edges to make them look like handlebars. His northern mother, with the big bosom, hands Tommasino a bag full of food, like Rosa did for me. Alcide comes into the compartment with me and puts my suitcase and violin case on the rack. Derna holds my hand from outside the window. She doesn't say a thing, and neither do I. We go on singing our song even as the train pulls away, and Derna's fingers slip out of mine, and she gets smaller and smaller till her blouse is just a tiny white dot. I'm all alone again, in the midst of all these kids.

"What's wrong?" Tommasino asks. "Are you homesick already?"

I don't answer. I turn my head the other way and pretend to go to sleep.

"It's normal," he says. "We are split into two halves now."

I don't feel like talking. Tommasino opens up his jacket and shows me some stitching his northern mother has put in. He says she has sewn money into the lining, so that if he misses them, he can go back up north again.

"Night-night, Tommasì."

"Take care, Amerì."

I look up and check that my violin is still on the rack. In my mind, I run through the exercises Maestro Serafini has taught me, so I'll still be able to do them when I go back up north. Carolina will be able to teach me a few more. Maybe Mamma will let me go to the Conservatory when she sees how good I am. That way, when I go back to Modena, Alcide will invite Serafini to see my progress. In the meantime, my little calf Amerigo will have become a bullock, I'll be able to help Rivo water the animals, Nario will have learned to walk, and we'll all go to our secret hideout and carve his name next to ours.

Then I pat the lining of my jacket and find there's no hidden pocket sewn in there. Derna hasn't given me the money to come back. And in a few weeks the calf probably won't even remember me. Neither will they. They'll chat about this and that, sitting around the kitchen table. About the new kids that will have arrived, maybe. Or about a cow that is expecting. The next calf will get the name of another kid.

All the things I had have already gone: my birthday cake, top grades in math from Mr. Ferrari, our light signals in the window, the smell of pianos, the taste of freshly baked bread, Derna's white blouse. I get my violin down from the rack and open the case. I brush my fingers along the strings and read my name on the label: Amerigo Speranza. Then I think about Carolina's face when I show it to her. With this thought, the sadness in my belly is a little less painful, and, as I gradually move farther away from my life now, and closer to my life before, I feel a little happiness taking its place. Derna's, Rosa's, and Alcide's faces begin to transform into those of Mamma Antonietta, Pachiochia, and Zandragliona.

Tommasino is right. We are split into two halves now.

Part Three

28

THE TRAIN PULLS INTO THE STATION. I STICK my head out the window to see if I can spot Mamma Antonietta, but she isn't there. The stench of the crowd catches in my nose. It's like Rosa's animal pen, without the cows.

As we get off the train, Tommasino finds his family almost immediately. Until yesterday, I saw him arm-in-arm with his mustached babbo and northern mother, but now here he is, hand in hand with his older brothers and Donna Armida, his southern mamma. I think the same might be true for me; that as soon as I lay eyes on Mamma Antonietta, everything that has happened over these months will vanish into thin air. Which makes me want to jump right back on the train and go up north again.

But then, behind a fat man carrying two brown suitcases, I see my mamma. She has her good dress on, the flowery one, and her hair is hanging loose over her shoulders. She hasn't spotted me yet, but I've seen her. She's looking around, her eyes filled with fear, like when she used to tell me the story about the bombing that killed Grandma Filomena.

I run as fast as I can and clasp her from behind, my face on her back, my hands on her belly, and my arms tight around her hips. Mamma Antonietta must think I'm a thief. She shoves me away with her elbow. Then, when she turns around, she says, "You'll be the death of me, you will!" She crouches down, touching my face, my arms, my legs, checking that everything is in place. Our eyes are at the same level. Finally, she puts a hand on my cheek and says, "My, how you've grown. They say weeds grow the fastest!"

The whole way home, I'm the only one talking. Mamma walks in silence, looking straight ahead, without asking me anything.

"When the calf was born, they called it Amerigo like me," I tell her, showing off a little.

"Sure," she says, giving me a soft cuff on the ear. "One animal wasn't enough for them, they needed two with the same name." I try to detect whether she's smiling underneath. I decide she probably is.

I go on chatting about the house, the food, the school, but I don't know whether she's really listening. It feels like when you have a dream and the next morning you tell everyone about it, but nobody cares at all and so you slowly realize the whole thing was just in your mind, and that by lunchtime you will have forgotten everything. Except that this isn't a dream. My suitcase is packed full of stuff I've been given, I have Alcide's violin in its case, I have new clothes and shoes on. All these things are for real.

We finally reach our street. It's quite hot. All the women are outside their front doors, fanning themselves. Mamma opens the door and puts my suitcase down. I clutch my violin case because I don't know where to put it. I don't have a room of my own. I don't even have my own bed. I look under Mamma's bed, where Capa 'e Fierro's things used to be stashed, and see that it's empty under there.

"Capa 'e Fierro's gone," Mamma says.

"Did the police take him away again?" I ask.

"No, he left with his wife and children. From now on, it's just you and me. We need to get on with things on our own. . . . Do you want to eat something? Are you hungry after your journey?" she asks.

She puts a cup of milk on the table and some stale bread from yesterday. It was what I used to eat every day, but now it feels scant. My whole life has shrunk again. I open my suitcase and take out the jams, the soft cheese, the hard cheese, the sausage, the mortadella, the cheese-and-salami pie, wrapped up in the yellow-and-white-striped tea cloth, which still smells of Rosa's kitchen, the fresh pasta that Rosa made yesterday morning that I'd broken the egg into and helped her mix, covered in white flour up to my elbows. It feels like a year has gone by, not a day.

I take all these things and lay them out on the table, as if we were having a party. They hardly fit on our kitchen table. Mamma starts touching and smelling everything, like she does at the vegetable market to check things are fresh.

"Look what the world has come to . . . now it's the kids bringing food home for the mothers."

I dip the old bread into the milk and then I spread a little of Rosa's jam on the top, just a teaspoon.

"Try it. It's made with fruit from their trees."

Mamma shakes her head.

"You have it. I'm not hungry."

She unpacks my clothes, notebooks and school textbooks, pens and pencils.

"You were already Nobèl before you left. Don't tell me they've turned you into a musician up there, too?" she says, pointing at the violin.

I open the violin case, and the smell of wood and glue in Alcide's workshop hits me.

"My babbo up north made this specially for me, with his own hands. He wrote my name in it, see?"

"I can't read," she says.

"Do you want to hear what it sounds like?"

Mamma looks up at the ceiling.

"Listen to me, boy. You only have one father, and he left to go seek his fortune. When he comes back with bags of gold, you can take some presents up to that family, and we won't need to ask any more favors of anyone."

She takes the violin out of my hands and looks at it as if it were a strange critter that might bite her from one moment to the next.

"In the meantime, though, we need to get on with things on our own. I spoke to the cobbler, and he said he'd take you on to help with the shoe repairs. First, you'll work for nothing, to learn the trade. Then, after a while, when you get better at it, he'll pay you something, and who knows where it could go from there . . . ?"

I rub my eyes, as if the dream wasn't my life up north, but this one down here, and when I wake up, I will find myself on Derna's big bed, the light shining through the window, making stripes on the sheet. That would be reality.

"Mr. Ferrari says I'm good at math."

"And does this Mr. Ferrari say he'll send you money every month to keep us going?" she yells. "Did you tell your teacher that your mother is not a common thief? That there are honest, hardworking people here, too?"

She goes around the room picking up everything I brought with me: the clothes, the notebooks, the food. I don't know what she's going to do with it.

"Put that thing down now. You won't be needing it," Mamma says. The violin and its case with my name in it are shoved under the bed. I don't say a thing. I put my hand in my pocket and twizzle Luzio's marble around in my fingers. It's all I have left.

29

ONNA ANTONIETTA, GOOD MORNING!" ZAN-
dragliona says, sweeping through the door with a big, fat
smile on her face. "Can I borrow this little urchin for a while and
take him home? I want to see whether he still remembers how we
make onion frittata down here, or whether he's forgotten everything while he was up there."

"You're quite right. He's even forgotten who his mother is up
there. He hasn't given me a smile since he set foot in this house. All
he's interested in now is the violin and adding up and taking away."

"What are you talking about, Donna Antonietta? You know
kids. They're just whims. Then they go away," Zandragliona says,
winking at me.

"Come over to my place for a while. I'll refresh your memory
with a little fizzy water made with a sachet of Idrolitina . . ."

Her ground-floor apartment hasn't changed a bit.

"Is my tin of treasures still there?" I ask, pointing at the tile
under which I'd hidden it.

"Nobody's touched it," Zandragliona says, pouring the sachet of bicarbonate into the water to make it go fizzy.

We sit there in silence, but it's nice anyway.

"Mamma doesn't love me anymore," I say, breaking the silence. "First, she sends me up there for my own good, and now she has it in for me. I want to go back up there where they treat me properly and caress me.

"Listen, kid," Zandragliona says as she cuts the onions. "Your Mamma Antonietta has never had a caress in her life, and that's why she doesn't have any to give. She's taken care of you all these years, and now that you're growing up, you'll have to take care of her. The war took many things away from us, all of us. She lost a son, and I lost my Teresinella."

I'd heard the story on the street, but she'd never told me herself.

"How did it happen?" I ask.

"She was only sixteen. She was one of my sister's four children and she'd come to live with me. I brought her up as if she were my own daughter. She was beautiful and very bright. After the Armistice, she joined the partisans, because she had fallen in love with one of them. She went back and forth across the enemy line, carrying information. Once, while she was on an assignment, she stole a revolver from a German soldier who had been killed in action. He didn't look like a German when he was dead, she said. He just looked blond and startled. She didn't tell anyone she had stolen the revolver, because the men would have taken it away from her. She kept it to herself. I was the only one who knew.

"When the partisans attacked the German car in the Vomero quarter, on September 27, 1943, Teresinella had left the house early in the morning. Nobody knew why, but I understood. I looked all over the city for her, and that was when I found out that the whole area was being barricaded by the insurgents. When I got there, I could smell the gunpowder in the air. I looked for Teresinella, but the air was thick with gray smoke, and I couldn't see a thing. It was a matter of seconds: I looked up and there was Teresinella with the revolver in her hand, shooting from behind a barricade as if she were a grown-up man. Every shot made her body shake, but she went on. I shouted, 'Get down! Get down from there!' Teresinella looked at me and smiled, but she didn't come down. She stayed up there, surrounded by men, shooting and shaking. Then there was the last shot, the loudest. After that, Teresinella didn't shake anymore. She didn't move anymore. Two days later, the Germans retreated. The city had been liberated by its own citizens. But Teresa never knew."

The onions on the cutting board have been reduced to thin slices, and Zandragliona's eyes are red and brimming with tears. She gets the green-checked tablecloth out and the napkins. All you can hear between us is the clatter of plates and glasses.

When I get back home and open the door, Mamma Antonietta, who has been sleeping, wakes up with a start.

"Ah, it's you! Come here. Come and lie down a little with me . . ."

I go and lie down on the bed. It's three in the afternoon and Mamma's in her nightgown. Her eyes look a little tired, but she's beautiful anyway. More beautiful than before, in fact. Her raven-black hair is longer and shinier and her mouth is dark pink, even though she doesn't use lipstick; she has never had any makeup. I think about Derna's pale skin and blond hair.

Mamma rests her head on the pillow. She reaches her hand out and ruffles my hair. I cuddle up next to her and take in her smell again. I remember that I've missed her. I fall asleep and dream

30

W E DON'T WALK TOGETHER ANYMORE, WITH Mamma one step ahead and me one behind. It's just me, now. Sometimes Tommasino.

Life has gone back to normal, but nothing is like before. The summer is almost over, but it's still hot. In the morning, I go to Mariuccia's cobbler father's workshop. I'm learning to use glue and little nails to resole shoes. The nails leave dimples in my fingertips, replacing the calluses I had from playing the violin. Mariuccia's brothers look askance at me. There's not much work, and I'm stealing theirs. Mariuccia sends a letter every now and again, written in her big, slanting cursive. Her cobbler father can't read, of course. He didn't even open her first letters. Then he asked me to read them. I was happy to, because I wanted to know what Mariuccia was doing, and to remember the things I used to do when I was up there.

Every time I opened one of her letters, though, her voice seemed more and more distant. She wrote because she felt she had to, but you could tell she didn't care one bit about us. They made me feel sad in my belly and so I stopped reading them. I told the family that reading hurt my eyes, and it wasn't a complete lie.

Mamma Antonietta has started taking in sewing again. She mends and alters clothes for ladies who live in Via Roma or the Corso. When she's busy, I go over to Zandragliona's place. But it's hot there, too. So I go out and look for Tommasino. We go around town, finding shade in the narrow alleyways. We go to Prince Sangro's chapel to see the skeletons. We go to the market and hide among the stalls. We go to the music Conservatory.

This is where I'd met Carolina, the day I'd sat here listening to the instruments playing inside. A porter had come out and shooed me away. He'd thought I wanted to steal an instrument to sell to the Americans. He'd said a flute and a clarinet had already disappeared. I'd been so ashamed, I felt like crying. I'm not a thief. I'd told him I was there to listen to the music. It was just then that Carolina had walked out the door. She'd looked over at me and, without even knowing who I was, told the porter I was her cousin, and that I was waiting for her. The porter had slunk away, giving me dirty looks and saying that in any case I wasn't allowed to sit out here. Carolina had smiled at me and pressed a coin into my hand. I'd taken it badly.

"I'm not here to beg," I'd said. "I'm not poor."

She'd smiled and said, "Go buy a pastry, then."

I'd said I wasn't hungry and that I'd been working.

"Really?" she'd said. "What work do you do? Let's hear."

"Me? I reconstruct music," I'd answered, dead serious.

After that day, she'd started to take me inside the big theater with her. She had a relative who was an usher there, and would let her into rehearsals and sometimes even performances. We'd hide up in the royal box and wait for the musicians to pick up their instruments. Then, when it was all dark, the conductor would draw two circles with his arms, as if he were embracing the whole orchestra, and each musician would start playing by himself, although the music came out all together.

SINCE COMING BACK, EVERY NOW AND AGAIN, I SIT outside at the usual time, waiting for Carolina to come out. But she never does. One day, I asked a friend of hers I had met, and she told me Carolina didn't go to the Conservatory anymore because her father had lost his job, and she and her brothers had to go to work after school. I asked her whether she knew where Carolina lived, but she didn't. She thought maybe in Via Foria, but she wasn't sure. So Tommasino and I walked up and down Via Foria the whole afternoon, the sun beating down on our heads, but we didn't bump into her. Eventually, we turned back and started walking home. We stopped in front of Pachiochia's apartment and saw that the photo of the mustached king was no longer there. Nor was there a picture of Comrade Lenin. We remembered when she had come north and climbed up onto the stage in her red, white, and green sash. We agreed, without saying a word, to take the Corso rather than go home, and walked all the way to the station. We walked partly in silence and partly chatting about things we'd done up north.

We were like Trombetta, the crazy veteran who begged in Piazza Carità. He'd been wounded in the head by a piece of shrapnel, and when he'd gotten home, he told the same story every single day, but nobody wanted to listen. "That's enough," they'd say. "We've already lost the war. Do you want us to lose our peace, too?" Tommasino and I were the same. At first, everyone asked us questions: Where were you? What language do they speak up there? What do they eat? Is it cold? But then they would start teasing us whenever they came near us. "Here come the two northerners," they would jeer. In the end, we only told our stories to each other on our way to the station.

We learned all the timetables and platforms by heart. Every time a train was set to leave for Bologna, I'd look at the people getting on with their heavy suitcases and tired expressions, and I'd remember throwing our coats out the window, the apple in my pocket, and Mamma Antonietta disappearing slowly into the distance, as the train moved farther and farther away. I think back to when it was us on the train: me, Mariuccia, and Tommasino, the blond kid with gaps in his teeth, the children who were scared we were going to Russia, and the ones who had no idea what they were doing on that train.

"Does your babbo with the mustache write to you still?" I ask Tommasino, hoping he says no. Since I got back, I haven't gotten one letter. Derna said she would write to me once a week; three months have gone by, and not one letter has arrived.

"Always," Tommasino says happily. "He sends us packages, too. All their produce: oil, wine, salami. And photographs of everyone."

He's quiet for a while, and then he looks at me.

"What about you? Still nothing?"

I shrug and don't answer.

"Mamma goes every two weeks to pick up the packages and the letters at Maddalena's house. They're always there, they never fail to get in touch . . ."

"Tommasì, let's get on the train now. Right now. This one's

leaving. We'll get to Bologna and then take the bus, and we'll go back to how we were before!"

Tommasino looks at me to see whether I'm being serious or not, and then bursts out laughing.

"Come on, let's go home," he says in the end. "Let's go and ask Pachiochia for two lire so we can buy a sfogliatella pastry to share." He turns around and heads toward the exit. I stay behind gazing at the train, until I hear the whistle blow.

31

I WALK ALONG THE CORSO LOOKING AT THE SHOES. They're all old, worn out, full of holes, or resoled. Since I started working at the cobbler's, I see people's shoes every day: some are worn out around the toes, others have a broken heel; some have holes, others have been deformed by their wearer's feet. Every pair of shoes belongs to a poor person; every hole is a mishap; every broken heel, a fall. It's not a game anymore.

My shoes are hurting. Alcide bought me a brand-new pair but now they rub against my heel. The shoes are still good. It's my heel that's grown, that's no good. But I carry on walking. They've just put up the lights for the Piedigrotta Festival. A group of boys playing tambourines and party blowers is parading behind me, singing songs that have been chosen for the competition this year. On the other sidewalk, five or six girls dressed as peasants for the traditional Epiphany procession join in the singing. The boys turn to send the girls kisses, and the girls turn the other way pretending not to notice. There are stalls laden with lupin beans and *taralli* crackers. Kids in their best clothes stroll with their parents, and the farther down the Corso I walk, the thicker the crowd gets, like that morning when Mamma Antonietta took me to the station. The crowd is massive, people are pushing me this way and that. It's like a wild animal. When I was at Derna's and Rosa's, the streets were never as full as this. I was used to it before, but now I'm almost scared by the crush. There are lots of people with painted faces or masks. I start running away from the crowd toward Via Mezzocannone, and then walk up the hill to Piazza Domenico Maggiore.

Without realizing it, I have somehow ended up outside the Conservatory. The violin is still sitting under my bed, and I haven't played it since I got back. Mamma Antonietta says my practicing gives her a headache.

Music wafts out the open windows. The air is still and stifling. I sit on the steps and close my eyes. I hear my name being called from far away.

"Amerigo, Amerigo, is that really you?"

Carolina crosses the road, and her violet smell hits me. She's not carrying her violin.

"You stopped coming to wait for me after my lessons. I was worried . . ."

She looks at me as if I'm a ghost who has returned after a long time. Maybe I am just that.

"I went to a place that is very far away," I say. She's grown, too. She looks almost like a signorina.

"Was it nice?"

"They taught me to play the violin. I could choose any instrument I wanted, but I thought of you."

She turns away. Maybe she doesn't want to be my friend anymore. But I soon realize it's because she's sad.

"My violin's at the pawnshop. My father lost his job, and there are four of us kids. We all have to contribute. I'd have stayed up there if I'd been in your place."

"You can play my violin if you like," I said. "In exchange, you can give me a few lessons. What do you say?"

I smell her perfume before I feel the kiss on my cheek.

We start heading toward my house. There's a light breeze, and every now and again, in waves, I smell the violets, and it makes my stomach tingle.

"Have you ever been back to the theater?" I manage to ask her as we walk up the hill.

The crowd on Via Toledo is even more jammed together than before. They are all snaking toward Piazza del Plebiscito to see the church completely covered in festival lights and the papier-mâché floats preparing to set off. Pachiochia told me that the rain had ruined many of them and that only four were still standing. One of them, she said, was called "North-South," and it had been built by the festival committee to celebrate our journey north on the train.

There are so many people crammed into Via Roma that it looks narrower than our alleyway. I grab Carolina's hand and start walking up the street in the Spanish Quarter where I live, terrified of losing her in the crowd.

When we get to my apartment, I pause. I'm a little ashamed to invite her in. I open the door, and Mamma isn't there. Carolina comes in behind me. She looks around and doesn't say a word. I don't know what her house is like. I'd like to tell her that at

Derna's house I had a room of my own, with a desk and a view of the fields. But I don't say anything and crouch down by the bed.

I lie on the floor and, after all that heat, I feel the cool of the tiles refreshing my whole body. I stretch both arms under the bed. There's nothing there. I get up, turn on the light, and look again. My violin is not there. There's nothing under the bed.

"Maybe Mamma moved it," I say, blushing bright red. "So that it wouldn't get ruined."

I pretend to look around the room. Then I crawl under the bed again.

"It's getting late," Carolina says. "I really need to go. You can show me another time."

I think about the day I'd gotten the present, wrapped in colored paper. I think about when I had opened the case, and the smell of wood and glue hit me for the first time. It wasn't like the glue at the Pizzofalcone cobbler's. They were two very different workshops. And I think about when Derna had produced Mamma Antonietta's letter that I'd waited so long for and that she'd had Maddalena write for her. All of a sudden, Tommasino's words come back to me: those letters and packages that arrive every two weeks. I brush away my tears and run out of the alleyway.

32

MADDALENA LIVES AT THE TOP OF THE PALLO-netto steps at Santa Lucia. There are five or six kids playing tag on her street. I used to be like them before I got on the train. They look at me and I look back at them.

"Do you know where a woman called Maddalena lives?" I ask the biggest one.

"The Commie, you mean?"

I nod.

He strides up to me and stares straight into my eyes. I don't flinch. Then he's suddenly on top of me. Another, shorter boy with a red birthmark on his face leaps onto my shoulders. The big one grabs me by the shirt and shoves me down onto the ground hard. I try to get up, but there are five or six boys holding me down.

"You're one of those kids that got to go on the trains, right?"

I don't answer.

"Every day there's one of you here. They have her write letters and go home with food packages. They've struck gold!"

"And we're here at the ready," the short brat with the birthmark on his face says. The big one stares him down and the short one shuts up.

"This is our street. Anyone who comes this way has to give us their stuff. And that means you, too," the big one says, sending me sprawling with a kick, just as I was getting up.

"Do you get it? Yes or no?"

"Nobody's sent me anything," I say, and it's true.

"We'll see when you come out," the big one says, signaling that I can get up now. "Go to the Commie, go on. We'll be waiting for you when you come out."

I run up the steps and knock on the door labeled Criscuolo. I hear Maddalena's steps approaching, and then I see her face appearing behind the door. I slip in as quickly as I can, scared that the gang might have followed me up here. She doesn't say a thing. She just looks and smiles.

"I'm Amerigo," I say. "The one who was left until last."

"I know," she says. "Sit down."

I sit in an armchair with worn armrests. What has gotten into me to come all the way up here? This woman doesn't even remember who I am, and that gang will have my scalp as soon as I leave. Maddalena gets up and goes into the other room. When she comes back, she's holding a package of envelopes. The letters are all there, sealed inside, with the stamps on the outside.

"Here they are," she says. "I think they're all here."

I look at her, dumbstruck.

"I've been waiting for you for three months. Have you been very busy?"

"You've been waiting for me? To do what?" I ask, still confused.

"At least, send an answer. These people looked after you for six months. They treated you like their son, and they keep writing to you. Your mother said you would come to get the letters, but Christmas has been and gone, and now it's Epiphany, and no one's the wiser."

She hands me the package of letters. They contain Derna's words, Rosa's, Alcide's, my northern brothers'. All of a sudden, their voices explode in my head, their faces, their smells. Everything. I leap out of the armchair, and all the letters fall onto the floor.

"They sent you food packages, too, but nobody came, so I distributed them to others in need. It was a pity to waste them!"

I can't speak. I sit on the floor and pick up one of the envelopes with Derna's name on it, addressed in her tiny, tidy handwriting. She's so good at it, and I hold on to it tight with both hands, so tight that the envelope tears a little on one side. Then I get up and put it in my pocket. Maddalena comes up to me and reaches out to stroke my hair, but I pull my head away. I'm not the same kid who got on the train that November morning.

"Didn't she tell you?" Maddalena says, finally understanding.

If I stay one second longer, I'll start crying, and I don't feel like crying right now.

"Okay, it doesn't matter," Maddalena says. "Everything works out in the end. Let's get a pen and some paper, shall we, so we can answer?"

"Mamma's so mean," is all I can say, and I run out of the house.

I leave the letters there. I don't want to read them. There's no answer, anyway. Maybe it's for the best. It's better if they forget me altogether, and I them, and if they change the calf's name, too. Mamma's right. How do I fit in with them? Pianos, violins, animal pens, the partisan Befana witch, fresh pasta made with flour and water, Principal Lenin, the light signals, the coat with a red badge on it, Mr. Ferrari, me forming letters in a schoolbook, with the body in the thin space and the tail in the fat space, and him with his red and blue pen corrections. These things can't be contained on sheets of paper stuck into envelopes with stamps on top.

When I come down the steps, I show my empty hands to the gang of boys.

"Empty, see?" I say to the boys. "I'm going back to where I came from. I have nothing. I'm just like you. If anything, I'm even more screwed."

33

MAMMA'S MADE ME HER PASTA WITH BLACK olives and capers that used to be my favorite before I went north. I throw myself on the bed.

"What's wrong, aren't you hungry?"

I don't talk about the letters at all. I'm not angry with her, but I've lost my appetite, even though I haven't eaten since this morning. She comes and sits next to me on the bed, like Derna used to do every evening.

"Are you feeling okay?" she asks, her hand on my forehead. "You're not running a fever, but you look a little pale around the gills," she adds, as if she were a doctor. Looking over at the photo of my big brother, Luigi, on the bedside table, she says, "You're getting too thin." Then she gets up, sits down at the table, and says, "Your plate's here. Come and sit down."

"Where's my violin?" I say without moving from the bed.

She doesn't answer immediately. Then, after a pause, she says, "Come on, it's getting cold."

I don't move.

"I want to know where my violin is," I say, my voice shaking.

"You can't eat a violin. Violins are for people who already have food on their table."

"It was my violin. Where is it?" I shout this time.

"It's where it should be," she says, calmly, even though I shouted at her. She gets up from the table and comes to sit on the bed again next to me.

"With the money from the violin I've been able to buy food and new shoes for you, since your feet grow as fast as weeds. I've managed to set some aside, too, just in case. It's God's will," she says as she looks over at the boy in the photo with the dark black curly hair like hers. Then she does something she's never done before. She scoots over even closer and hugs me tight with both arms around me. I can smell her on my face and in my nose and eyes. She's warm; too warm and too sweet. I close my eyes and hold my breath.

"You need to pinch yourself and wake up from that dream, Amerì," she says. "Your life is here now. You wander around all day like you're sleepwalking; your thoughts are always someplace else. You look beat. That's enough now. Do you want to get sick, too?" She stares at me as she holds me close. "I did it for your own good."

I pull away from her embrace and get up from the bed.

She thinks she knows what's best for me, does she? Well, nobody knows. What if it was best for me to stay up north, like Mariuccia did, and never come back? What if it was best for me never to have left, and to have stayed here at home? What if it was best for me to learn music and play in the theater? I want to say all these things, but the only thing that comes to mind is that I'll never get my violin with my name in its case back.

"You're a liar . . ." I don't have time to finish the sentence before her slap lands on my cheek, so hard that my tongue is stuck between my teeth, and I can't say another word for the stab of pain.

34

I RUN OUT OF THE HOUSE AND DOWN THE STREET, taking the alleyways to avoid being swallowed up by the crowds. I run with the shoes Alcide bought for me rubbing the back of my heels. I run without looking back. I can hear the music coming from Piazza del Plebiscito. It is getting dark and all the festival lights are ablaze. The streets look as though they are made of light: the shapes of the buildings have been outlined with strings of colored bulbs that also run around the windows and walls. It feels like a city of stars in the middle of a pitch-black sky. I'd like to get lost, but I know these streets by heart. House by house, door by door. I follow the lights and run. I take Vico Figurelle at Montecalvario and turn into Via Speranzella, until I find myself at the Vico Tre Re in Toledo, right in front of the church where there's the chair of St. Mary Frances of the Five Wounds they say works miracles. Tommasino and I have been here often to listen to the stories, but we have never been inside.

The stories were always the same story, actually. Women arrived from all over the city, and even from outside, to beg the saint for a baby that didn't seem to be coming to them. So many women, every day, with their mothers or with other women in their family: a sister, a sister-in-law, a mother-in-law, whoever. Women from poor areas and women from rich families, too. Some people have too much, and some people have too little. Mamma Antonietta, who was dying of hunger, had my brother, Luigi, and then me, with no father, while these ladies in their colorful clothes and shiny shoes, with husbands and everything else, can't even have one child. If there were justice in this world, as Zandragliona always said, only people who could afford to would have kids.

OUTSIDE THE CHURCH OF SANTA MARIA FRANCESCA, there's a line of women even at this time of day. An old nun, with a wizened, colorless face, walks toward me. She probably wants to send me away, I think, but she takes my hand and leads me into a little room that smells of warmed-up old broth. She sits me down at a table with some other kids.

"Eat," she says. She must have mistaken me for an orphan from the soup kitchen. I eat the pasta, bread and tomato, and an apple. When I'm done, the old nun goes into the other room and sits on a stool in front of the chair, where women go to receive a baby by the grace of God. She takes each woman's hand in her own, and with the other one makes the sign of a cross over the woman's belly, right where the new baby will be. The women say a prayer, thank the old nun, and leave.

By the time I get out of the church, it is even darker, and the streets are almost empty. The few people still around are heading toward the sea at Mergellina to see the fireworks and hear the songs.

I wonder what Derna is doing at this moment. She's probably walking along the silent road, where all you can hear is the chirping of crickets. Maybe she's laying the table with a single place, for herself. Or maybe she's just gotten back after a meeting with the women factory workers and she's stopped over for dinner at Rosa's house, where the table is full and all the lights are on. I reach into the pocket of my pants and pat Derna's letter. Sadness hits me like a punch in the belly. So I keep walking down through the alleyways until I get to Via Roma, which is now deserted. Where have all those people gone? Where did they all vanish to in so little time? The only noise I hear is in the distance. There is music playing, shouting, and singing, but it sounds squeaky and off-pitch, like an instrument that hasn't been tuned. They need Alcide's tuning fork, I think. All of a sudden, I hear an explosion behind me. My knees wobble as I remember the sound of the bombs when they fell from the sky; when the sky was filled with gunfire instead of stars, and the explosions were shells dropped by airplanes, not air-bomb fireworks. I run like crazy, but my shoes are hurting. So I stop, turn around, and see them arrive.

The floats are setting off on their procession around the city, followed by the crowds. That's why the streets are so empty. They are gigantic and brightly lit. I'm under their spell, and so I stand still as the lights on the floats come closer and closer, getting bigger and bigger the closer they get, like trains when they pull into the station. As the first float passes in front of me, I can see it is a train. It's our float, the kids' float, the one that the women's committee had had built. The kids inside look just like us, but they're not us. The train looks real, too. But I know it's not real. It's all pretend, and I don't believe the lies anymore.

That's why I turn the other way, wrench my shoes off, and start running toward the Corso.

35

A T THE STATION THERE'S A REAL TRAIN. THE same as the one I took the first time, but with no kids inside. Everything is quiet and nobody is running back and forth. There are lots of men carrying suitcases, and a few families traveling together. And me. I can't hear the music from the floats anymore, nor the air-bomb fireworks from the festival. The people around here don't look like they're in the mood for festivities.

A ticket collector comes by the platform. I ask him if the train is leaving. He says, "Of course it's leaving, do you think the trains are here just to look good?" Then he asks me what I'm doing at this hour all alone, and I tell him I have to go to Bologna with my mother, my father, and my big brother, Luigi; that we are going to visit an aunt in Bologna, and that my parents have sent me to check if we're on the right train. The man takes his cap off and dries his brow with the sleeve of his uniform.

"Watch it," he said. "There are bad people around at night. I'll take you to your mother."

I see a lady at the end of the platform and say, "She's just over there," as I turn, pretending I'm running toward her. When I look back, I see him walking in the other direction.

I put my shoes on again, even though they're rubbing badly. I go to stand near the lady who's not my mother and wait for the train doors to open. We climb up onto the train together, and the lady starts looking for her seat. I don't know where to sit. I'm scared the ticket collector from before, or another one, will find me and make me get off. The lady has two children, a little boy and a girl, only a little younger, in a stroller. The boy can hardly keep his eyes open and soon falls asleep in his mother's arms. I sit in the same compartment opposite them and stick my face against the window. The glass is cool and smooth. I like the cold on my face. Tomorrow, once I have gotten there, I will be able to fall asleep next to Derna. She'll tell me a story, and she'll talk to me about the problems of women factory workers, and we'll sing together, and she'll take me to the sea, but this time I won't go far. I won't get lost in the waves. This time I won't.

The mother opposite me takes her knitting out of her bag and slowly, knit one and purl one, she makes a pink cotton blanket, resting the end of it on her sleeping son's head. It reminds me of Mamma Antonietta when she gave me her old sewing tin, the one I hid at Zandragliona's house. They must both be looking for me high and low, and they won't find me anywhere. The station-master blows his whistle. I leap up and look out the window.

"Where are you going all on your own?" the mother with the two kids asks. "Have you run away from home?"

I'd like to tell her the truth, get off the train, and go home. But where is home now?

The train starts pulling out of the station slowly. I'll never get

Derna's letters. I'll never get my violin with my name in it back. But if I manage to get to the other end of the line, there's a chance I'll get another one.

So I sit back down and try to invent a lie. I think about the orphan's soup kitchen at the church and say, "Mamma's dead."

My tongue is burning with shame but I go on. I tell the lady that I'm going to meet an aunt of mine who lives in Modena. I pull Derna's letter out of my pocket and show it to her.

"Poor creature. Poor little lost soul," she says, with tears in her eyes.

She believes me. It's not the first time I've told a lie, but this one's different. I told it so convincingly, I almost believe it myself. And I'm scared it'll come true. The lady carries on consoling me.

"Everything will work out, poor little darling," she says, taking my face in her hands. I pull away because I can feel my cheeks flushing with shame.

Then my tiredness wins over my sadness, and I stretch my legs out on the empty seat next to her.

I dream that Tommasino and I are playing hide-and-seek in Prince Sangro's chapel, and I take the place of one of the two skeletons, the one with the bones and all the veins, so that he won't find me. Then I hear the steps coming closer and I chuckle, thinking Tommasino will have a shock seeing me there with the mummified skeletons. The steps come even closer, and Tommasino walks into the room where I'm hiding. But he can't find me. I'm so well hidden that nobody ever finds me. and I'm left there in the middle of the skeletons and stone statues that look alive. I shout, "I'm here, I'm here," hoping someone will find me, but nobody does.

My own shouts wake me up. I look out the window. It is pitch black, with no moon and no stars. The mother with the boy sleeping next to her opens her eyes and looks at me.

"What happened? Are you all right? You had a bad dream, that's all. Come over here."

I go over to her, and she pulls her hand out from under her son's sleeping head, dries my sweaty forehead, and smooths down my hair.

"Go back to sleep. Don't think about it. It's nothing. I'm here."

She makes a little space near her on the seat. Now there are three of us: her, the boy in her arms, and me. She picks up her knitting again and, one knit and one purl, the blanket grows long enough to cover me, too. I hope the sleep that runs through the mother's body into the son's, helping him sleep right through the night, will help me sleep too; help my eyelids go heavy and take all the thoughts out of my head. But it is not to be.

Part Four

1994

36

IT HAPPENED LAST NIGHT. YOU HAD MADE A *PASTA alla genovese* for the next day. You had washed your cutting board, ladle, and pan, and put them on the rack to dry. You had taken your apron off and left it, folded up, on the back of the kitchen chair. You had put your nightdress on, and let your hair loose. You never liked sleeping with your hair tied. Your hair had stayed almost completely black. You had gone to bed and turned the light off. The *genovese* had stayed on the stove, "resting" for the next day. You always used to say the *genovese* needed to rest. Then you had turned over and gone to sleep. You were resting, too.

They called me at dawn. When I answered on the third ring and heard the news, I realized I'd lived with the idea this might happen, looming over my life, like a curse. I didn't even manage to cry. My only thought was "There you go; the curse has finally come true." I said, "Yes, yes. I'll take the first flight down," and then I left. Now, alone in the night, you are the one that has gone. No other phone call will ever scare me again.

As I get off the plane, carrying my bag in one hand and my violin case in the other, I am engulfed in the heat. A slow bus deposits me in front of the arrivals hall, and I walk down the corridor to the automatic doors. They glide open, but there's nobody there to greet me. I walk toward the exit, while passengers flying to Munich are being invited to go to the gate.

A group of Spanish tourists approaches me asking for information. I pretend not to understand, otherwise I would have to confess I am a foreigner in my own city. I'm hot, and my shoes are hurting. A big blister has formed on my left heel and another, smaller one, on my right. My beige linen jacket sticks to my skin as soon as I emerge from the unnaturally cool air of the airport.

I flag a taxi and ask to be taken to Piazza del Plebiscito. The taxi driver tries to take my bag and violin case to put into the trunk.

"Not the violin," I say. "I'll keep that with me."

As we drive, I gaze out the window: stores, buildings, streets communicate nothing to me. The few times I'd been back, I'd always gotten everything done quickly and arranged a hasty meeting with you. I never set foot in your house. You were ashamed that I might be ashamed of you. We used to meet in Via Toledo, the one that was called Via Roma in my day, and I would treat you to lunch out. I would book a restaurant on the seafront. You liked it, even though the water still scared you a little, because for you the sea had always been dirty, damp, and diseased. You always used to say the sea had no purpose. Some of those times, Agostino had come, too. But only in the early days, when he still listened to you. Then, as he grew up, he started inventing excuses. He always said he was busy. It was for the best, I always thought. You wanted us to be more united. But I always wondered: What unites us?

I rest my head on the back of the seat in the taxi and close my eyes. My suit is clinging to my sweaty body, and the blisters on my heels throb painfully.

"Are you a musician?" the taxi driver asks.

"No," I lie. "I'm an actor." Then I remember the violin and tell him I'm playing the part of a violinist and carry it with me to get into character.

The taxi drops me off in the piazza, and I start walking along the road, which looks yellow in the sunlight. At the turning to go up to your street, I stop and wait. I'm not ready yet. Perhaps I never will be. I take a handkerchief out of my pocket. There are no tears, so I wipe my brow and set off.

37

A S I MAKE MY WAY UP THROUGH THE GRID OF narrow streets, I find that, rather than becoming more intense, the heat is mitigated by a cool breeze, emanating from the ground-floor tenement apartments that open onto the street. The shade reaches out from the buildings that face one another like mirror images on both sides of the street, crisscrossed with washing lines and clothes hanging out to dry, like a welcomingly cool cover. People stare at me as they would an outsider, with a suspicious air. I start walking faster, even though the street is rising steeply, and my shoes are rubbing against my heels. I avoid the gaze of all those people you used to meet every day, people you would greet and who would greet you back. I don't want to hear their voices. Sounds, voices, noises; ever since I was a boy, they would get stuck in my ears and never leave me in peace. People on my street were always singing, even when they were speaking. It was always the same music. It's never changed. I put my hands in my pocket to avoid any contact with their bodies and pat my wallet and driver's license to make sure they are still there. People have told me about being beaten up and robbed by gangs of kids here. Every time, I thought it could have been me; I could have been one of those kids in this city who grew up too fast but never became an adult.

When I reach the door of your house, my heart is in my throat. It's not only the emotion of being here after so many years away, or the pain of knowing you're there in that room, lying on the bed that we used to share, your loose hair still almost completely black. No, it's fear. Fear of dirt, of poverty, of need, of being an imposter, of living a life that's not mine and taking a name that doesn't belong to me. Over the years, my fear has learned to curl up into a corner of my mind, but it hasn't gone altogether; it's lurking at the margins of my conscience. Like now, standing in front of the closed door of your apartment. You weren't afraid of anything. You never lowered your gaze. Fear doesn't exist, you would say. It's your imagination. I've been telling myself the same thing all my life, but I've never convinced myself.

A big gray cat rubs against my legs and sniffs at my leather shoes. It must be Ciccio Cheese, our alley cat. I used to give it dry bread and a little milk, and you would shoo it away rudely. My memories deceive me, though. The cat arches its back, fluffs out its fur, and hisses at me. I rest my hand on the doorknob, but I'm no longer sure what I came here to do. It might be best to leave and be done with it.

An orange soccer ball bounces down the street on the loosely fitting cobbles, hits my knee, and rolls farther down, ending up behind the wheels of a scooter parked in front of the apartment building opposite yours. A kid comes running after it, and I point to where the ball is hiding. His jeans are fashionably ripped at the knees, he has one shoelace undone, and a faded T-shirt. He smiles, with the ball in his hand, and runs on down the street. He looks happy. Maybe I was happy once, but it was a long time ago. As I watch him disappear, the ancient, worn-out fabric of my memories that I'd always stretched to keep pace with the present all of a sudden becomes the right size, fitting my eyes with millimetric precision. I look back and see myself running down the street with my red hair, one missing milk tooth that the "tooth mouse" had taken in exchange for a piece of cheese, and my knees full of bruises and grazes.

38

I KNOCK QUIETLY, BUT NOBODY COMES TO THE door. I try pushing, and the door opens. There is very little light filtering through the half-closed shutters. The table and chairs, the kitchen nook, the bathroom at the end, the bed in a dark corner. It takes a second to take in the whole apartment. Everything is almost exactly as it used to be. The rush-bottomed chairs, the hexagonal tiles on the floor, the same ancient brown table we had back then. The television set, with the lace doily you made with your own hands on top, the radio I gave you once for your birthday. Your flowery day-coat hanging on the coat rack, the white bedspread crocheted by your mother, Filomena, bless her soul. You are the only thing missing.

On the stove, the pan with the *genovese* sauce is "resting." The smell of steeped onion fills the minuscule apartment, proof that you were planning to be alive today, that you should be here in your place to eat it.

I circuit the whole place in a few steps. It takes so little to sum up your life. Anybody's life, perhaps. I can't bring myself to touch anything. Your slippers worn out at the toes, your hairpins, the mirror that has received your image for so many years, watching it age day by day, in minimal increments. It feels sacrilegious to leave your few possessions unguarded. The damp circle under the basil pot on the windowsill, your stockings, the right leg darned repeatedly over the big toe, hanging over the shower curtain, the liquor bottles on the dresser filled with pink, yellow, and blue colored water because they "look nice that way." I'd like to carry everything out to safety as if you and the whole house were about to drown. On the dresser, next to your nail scissors and hairpins, there's a little ivory comb. I stroke it, pick it up, weigh it in my hand, and slip it into my pocket. Then I take it out again and put it back where it was. The place you had given it. I feel like a thief, like a Peeping Tom, like somebody who has wormed his way into your intimacy and sees things that have not been laid out for him. I open the front door wide and let the sun come in to light up the dark room. Before locking up, though, I go back into the kitchen. I trace your footsteps as far as the pan left on the stove. The butcher, opposite, for the meat, "make sure it's a nice tender cut"; the vegetable man on the corner, at the end of the alleyway, for the onions, carrots, and celery; you breaking the ziti by hand into an earthenware casserole. The onion sizzling in olive oil until it goes transparent, simmering with a sprinkle of wine to balance the acidity, time and heat disintegrating the meat, as with all flesh, the water boiling and the pasta gradually softening until it reaches its perfect starchy consistency.

I look at my watch. It's lunchtime, and it feels like you've been cooking for me, for when I get home. I lift the lid, grab a fork, and grant you your dying wish.

I finish the pasta, wash the pan, and leave it to dry. Then I shut the door behind me and take the same way back, all the way down to the main road. The sound of my footsteps on the black paving stones, hanging laundry dripping from above, Vespas parked in the alleyways, like sleeping horses outside the apartments, wide-open doors and windows giving out onto the street, making it hard to preserve decency and not to peer inside and spy on the crowded lives inside.

A woman I don't know comes out of her ground-floor apartment. Her face is still young, but it has been aged by fatigue. Her black hair is hanging loose over her shoulders. She stares at me, squinting in the dazzling light, shading her eyes with one hand.

"You're Donna Antonietta's grown-up son, bless her soul. The violinist . . ."

"No, I'm a nephew," I say and walk on. I don't want to be a part of this neighborhood, with all its voracious meddling. I don't like this woman I don't even know talking about you as if you were dead. She follows me, a few steps behind.

"They took her away this morning. It's the heat, you know. They couldn't keep her here, the house is too small and the temperature is going up, they said it on TV. Can you hear me, or not?"

I stop and turn around, touching my temple.

"I'm deaf in one ear," I lie.

"Ah, sorry," the woman says, glaring at me suspiciously.

"Tomorrow morning, there's the funeral mass, at eight thirty, in the church of the saint, you know the one," she says. She stares at me diffidently a little longer and then goes back into her house, shouting after me, "You tell her son, then."

She's telling me out of respect for you, I know. Because you spent your whole life, and even your death, in this alleyway. She's not doing it for me. I'm the son who ran away. The one who never came to see you.

Rather than heading straight for Via Toledo, I decide to take a shortcut through the narrow streets to escape the heat. I lose myself in the shrines, with their candles and flowers, in the dark faces, the crooked teeth, the hoarse voices, and, without meaning to, I end up in front of the church where that evening the miracle-working nun fed me pasta, bread and tomato, and an apple, and where tomorrow morning the neighbor said my mother's funeral mass will be held. I stand in front of the church for a few minutes without going in. I move my lips pretending to say my prayers, but what I'm really thinking is that this is where I ran away from, and this is where I have returned. Except this time, you are the one who has run away without saying goodbye. And you won't be coming back.

39

I GO BY THE MAIN SQUARE AGAIN AND WALK DOWN to the seafront where the best hotels are; I've stayed in a couple. You used to tease me. "So, you've made money," you would say. "Weeds grow so fast." I wanted to buy you a house, a normal house with stairs, a balcony, and an intercom. You always said no. You didn't want to move.

"You're the one that travels; I stay in one place. Your brother Agostino has been trying to persuade me to move in with him and his wife up in the Vomero quarter. He's so generous, you know . . . you should see their house, the furniture . . . and what a view!"

You never wanted to see my house in Milan. Not even Derna's house in Modena, all those years I was there, nor after that, when I was studying at the Conservatory. Maybe you were scared of the train. I never asked you, and now I can't ask you. We loved each other from a distance. That's what I think. I wonder whether that's what you thought.

I stop in front of one of the most expensive hotels. I push the glass door open and I'm struck by a wall of cold air that makes my sweat go clammy. I ask at the reception for a room.

"Have you made a reservation?"

"No."

The receptionist looks askance at me.

"I'm afraid we're fully booked, sir."

He's wearing gold-rimmed glasses, what little hair he has left combed and gelled back, and he has an air of importance about him, as if he had the keys to paradise in his pockets, rather than the keys to a hotel suite. I suppose for him they're the same thing, ultimately.

"My daughter had a baby last night, and I've come to see my new grandchild," I say, handing him a generous tip in the hope a room will suddenly become available.

"I see, sir. I'll see what I can do."

He asks a liveried bellboy to take my bag and violin.

"Not the violin," I say. "This stays with me."

He leans imperceptibly across the reception desk and eyes me over the rim of his glasses, creasing his forehead and eyebrows into a frown.

"How many nights are you planning to stay?" he asks in a whisper.

I spread my arms, my palms facing up, as if to say "Who knows?" and he nods sympathetically.

"I've found a well-appointed room for you, sir, with a seafront view," he says, handing me the key. "Congratulations!" he adds, as I hand him my ID. "I'll have you accompanied to your room right away, Mr. Benvenuti."

The bellboy takes me up a few floors, unlocks the door, and asks whether the room is to my satisfaction. I nod and give him a tip. I rest the violin case on the bed, take a tour of the room, and open the door onto the balcony. I stand there in the current created by two qualities of air: the refrigerated air in the room and the sweltering air rising from the sidewalk two floors down. I'm exhausted. A fatigue borne of distance, as if I'd walked all the way here from Milan. As if all the years that have gone by, since I ran away and stole onto that train, were weighing down on me. I take my jacket off, roll my shirtsleeves up, and take my violin out of its case. I look out from the little balcony and stand there gazing at the sea, a blue line drawn like a border along one side of the city only. The gulf embraces the whole city in its arms, curving so gently that I'm almost sorry I've never been able to reciprocate and embrace you, Mamma. It feels as though everything has been a misunderstanding, a mutual betrayal, since that evening I called you a liar and ran to the station.

That night I slept in the arms of another mother. I can't even remember her name, or perhaps I never knew it. I told her you had died, and I was on my own. When the conductor came in at dawn, she said we were all her children, me and the other two, and he left. She bought me a bus ticket to Modena and waited until she'd seen me waving out the back window.

When Rosa saw me at the door, tears came to her eyes. She couldn't believe I had gotten back on my own, without telling anyone anything. Then Derna arrived and immediately called Maddalena. She said you must be looking for me all around the neighborhood, and that you must be dying of fright. I remembered the photo on your bedside table of my big brother, Luigi,

40

I STAY IN THE HOTEL ROOM, THE AIR-CONDITIONING on at full blast. I do nothing. I'm simply waiting for time to pass until tomorrow morning. A scream from two floors down on the street pierces the silence of the early afternoon.

"Carminiè!"

I go out onto the balcony and look down. There's a group of five kids pacing in front of the hotel. They stop and turn back again. The oldest looks about twelve, while the youngest can't be any older than seven. I observe them for a while. They look like a gang. They are tailing tourists, aiming for a small payoff or perhaps a little scam. The youngest, with jet-black hair, looks up at me. I look away and close the balcony door quickly to lock the voices speaking Neapolitan dialect out of the room, but it is too late. They have already insinuated their way into my head.

I pick up my violin from the bed and start playing an aria to chase the voices away, but it's no use. However muffled, the voices keep coming, bringing with them the sounds of my childhood that snap synapses in the back of my memory.

First, in the background, high-pitched children's voices, which are the violins, violas, and cellos, according to their age. Then the women's double bass, whose almost masculine throaty, gravelly voices play the bass line, beating the tempo of everyday life. And then there is the woodwind section, the stupidly chirpy, almost feminine sound of the men played by clarinets, flutes, and piccolos. Voices at the market, the endless gossip of housewives at the front doors of their tenement apartments, children chasing one another through the alleyways. Until I reach a voice that is buried in the innermost kernel of my recollection.

"Amerigo, Amerì! Come down here, quick. Go and get two lire from Pachiochia . . ."

It's your voice, Mamma.

41

I SPEND THE WHOLE AFTERNOON IN THE HOTEL room, waiting for the heat to dissipate. I haven't called Derna. I haven't called anyone. This way, it feels like I am keeping you alive, away from the finality of death, at least in other people's thoughts.

After sundown, I put my shoes on again and went out onto the seafront. I wasn't sure I was hungry. I walked back to your neighborhood, looking for a modest little trattoria, surrounded by smells of dinner on the stove, wafting from open windows. Four tables inside, in a windowless basement, and three outside, tables and chairs in the middle of the street. I stop just as the owner comes out in a T-shirt and white shorts, covered by a stained apron. He greets me as if he knows me, as if he's been expecting me, and sits me down at one of the unofficial tables, laid with a paper tablecloth and a chipped glass. The waiter brings me a greasy piece of paper with the menu of the day written on it. I gaze at it, amazed. I feel sure he has recognized me after all these years, though it doesn't seem possible. I soon realize the same scene is repeated with every customer. Everyone who walks past the place is welcomed with the same over-the-top shenanigans, which are part and parcel of the menu of the day. I look through the list and order a plate of pasta with potatoes and *provola* cheese, just like you used to make it, with the rind softened inside to give the dish extra flavor. My order comes almost at once. I take a sip of the red house wine and put the first spoonful in my mouth. The macaroni dissolves under my palate, the melted *provola* gluey. You always used to warn me to take small mouthfuls, otherwise I might choke, and then who would take me to the hospital? But I used to love cramming my mouth full of pasta, with its ambiguous flavor that united the sweetness of the potato and the saltiness of the cheese and continued to burn my lips after I'd finished the meal.

I eat with a hunger ill-suited to grief. Hunger is mean-spirited, though. It doesn't give a shit about good manners or loved ones. I wipe my mouth and ask for the check. The owner with the stained apron comes to the table and writes a few numbers in a column right on the paper tablecloth. He draws a line under them and tots up the total: nothing, a couple of thousand lire. I pull the notes out of my wallet and add a good tip.

"Do you have an apple?" I ask the host, who is already going back into the basement.

"Sorry, sir. What was that?" he says, peering out at me.

"An annurca apple," I say, a little embarrassed.

The host signals I should wait, his hand up, palm out, fingers wide. He goes down to the cellar and comes out two minutes later with a little red apple, like a compact heart.

"How much do I owe you?" I ask.

"What can I say, sir? I can't sell these. Nobody appreciates annurca apples anymore. They all want those big, tasteless ones. I keep these for people who know the difference."

"Well, thanks, then," I say, putting the apple in my pocket.

"Take care, sir," the host says, disappearing back into the trattoria.

As I walk back toward the hotel, the apple swells in my pocket, keeping me company, like the one you gave me that day as the train was leaving for Bologna, when I was surrounded by all those other children. You entrusted me to Maddalena Criscuolo's care. I wonder where Maddalena has got to. She was a fine young woman, and now she must be getting old. The same thing that has happened to me.

I left your apple to shrivel up and dry on my desk at Derna's house. I didn't want to eat it, because I wanted to keep your memory alive. But then, one day, it wasn't there any longer. Now I've done it again. I've let time go by, and now it's too late.

42

THE LIGHT OUTSIDE IS SO STRONG THAT THE dark inside feels even thicker. When I step inside, it is just beginning to rain, despite the sun, and the air in the church is hot and humid. You are there at the front, between the two naves, in the center. The wooden coffin is resting on a folding metal stand with wheels, as if you are a piece of furniture waiting to be moved.

There's a stench of damp mixed in with incense. A boy in a white tunic swings the golden censer, which emits puffs of gray smoke. When the priest appears, everyone stands, and the heat, stench, and dark make me feel faint. I don't know. It may be because you are there inside the coffin.

I get down on the kneeler; people may think I'm praying. The priest starts talking, but I don't hear a word. You never took me to church. God, Virgin Mary, and saints were never your strong point. Alcide never had anything to do with priests, either. My eyes slowly get used to the dark and I try to make out people's faces. In the front row, there are women dressed in black with their hair tied up tight. One of them has a white braid pinned in a coil around her head like a crown. She looks like a girl who has become very old. In the second row, on his own, there's a man with lanky gray hair stuck inside the collar of his shirt. He opens and shuts his eyes compulsively; at first, I think he is winking at me. His intermittent blinking forces me to observe him for a few seconds. In the interval between one blink and the next, I notice his eyes are dark blue. They have preserved a little of his youth. He looks tired, like everybody else here. Their faces are all pallid and strained, as if they'd been bleached. You didn't have any relatives. You only had me. And Agostino. I look all around the church, but I can't see him. So many years have gone by that I may not recognize him. There are not many of us here. Hardly two rows on each side of the nave. Few, but with good shoes on. A little worn out, but good. One and a half points.

The priest talks about you as if he knew you, and maybe he did. Perhaps in your old age you started going to church; maybe you went to mass on Sunday, made confessions, took communion from the priest's hand, and recited the rosary with the other women on your street. He may know you better than I do. I may be the person who knows you the least. The priest says you were a good woman, and that now God, in all his glory, has taken you to heaven together with all the angels and saints. Even though I am the outsider here, I still think you don't give a shit about angels or saints or paradise, because you were happy here in these alleyways, in your apartment, surrounded by people chanting. That's why you made *pasta alla genovese* and set it aside for the next day. Not so you could go away in glory with a host of saints. But then, death is a sneaky, high-handed thing. It smokes people out in the midst of their daily life, with all their little certainties and faults.

Every person perfects their own strategy for escaping death, but they are mistaken. They are mistaken when they believe they can cheat death by making *pasta alla genovese* for the next day. They are mistaken when they run away to another city, seeking a different destiny. They are mistaken when they think music will keep them out of harm's way. There is no safe harbor. Laughing through its teeth, death will ferret them out anyway, one by one, without distinction. And perhaps I, too, have come here to die of fear, of heat, of melancholy.

I feel like shouting, but my voice is locked in, and if I were to unlock it, tears would leak out with it. The priest says "sit," and we all sit. The priest says "stand," and we all stand. I feel like that trained monkey with the old man on the Corso. The priest invites us to take communion, and everyone files out of the benches to stand in line. The old man with long hair and a tic in his eyes stays in place. I stare at the painting of the saint on her deathbed: her face pale, her lips a vivid red. She doesn't look like she's about to die; rather, she looks like an attractive young woman getting ready to go to a party. I try to imagine that you are the saint in the painting and that you are lying there, nice and calm, with red lipstick on, ready for a party. Then, while everyone is still in line to take communion, I get up and walk toward the altar. I stop in the corner opposite the pulpit, take my violin out of its case, and start playing. The bow on the strings produces the sweetest, saddest music, which fills the church, which rises and falls, which in some passages sounds joyous and festive, rather than the lament of a mother for the absence of her son. It is an aria from Pergolesi's *Stabat Mater*, but there is no way you will recognize it. You never heard me play.

I go on playing for a few minutes, my left hand on the strings, my right hand on the bow. When the music comes to an end, the only sound is the rain outside. Everybody goes back to their places. The priest doesn't speak. I try not to look at the brown wooden coffin between the two naves, where you are floating motionless, but my eyes are drawn there, nonetheless. I would like to walk out of the church and leave immediately, this instant, without even going back to the hotel to pick up my things. As if I had never come back. As if you were still there, where I left you that very first day, on the other side of the train window, waiting.

The priest tells us the mass has come to an end, and we can go in peace, back to our homes. What peace? What homes? I feel like I have never had a home. A woman with silver-white hair in a man's cut goes up to your coffin, just before the four men, including the one with the tic, pick it up and put it on their shoulders to take out. The woman with the silver-white hair kneels down in silence for a few seconds, then closes her fist and raises it in the air. When she looks up at me, she smiles. So I, too, get up and walk to you and stroke the wood. It is hard and rough. I pull my hand away and put it in my pocket. Behind us, everybody files out. One by one, they bow to the altar and leave.

It has stopped raining, but the street is still wet and smells of earth and rotten vegetables. The woman with the silver-white hair walks toward me, her arms wide open. Behind her, the black-haired altar boy without his cassock and censer.

"Don't be embarrassed, Carmine," she says. "His last name is Speranza, just like yours."

I don't understand. I want to cut it short. I'm desperate to get away as fast as possible.

"You're mistaken, ma'am. My surname is Benvenuti," I say, and I start walking toward the main road. She calls me by my name and reaches up to place her hands on my shoulders. The boy looks at me without smiling, his eyes narrow, and all of a sudden, I realize he's the child with the gang of boys that was looking up at my balcony from the street.

The boy stares at me, his eyes screwed up small, as if the church, the damp, and your brown coffin being carried away by four strangers were all my fault. Or maybe I'm the one thinking it, not him. He's just a sad boy in front of a middle-aged man he has never seen before.

"You came by train," the old woman says, as if we were carrying on a conversation from before. Her voice gives her away more than anything else, but I don't answer her. Not even to tell her I never take the train, because that relentless clickety-clack of the wheels on the tracks, like a tongue persistently returning to a painful tooth, reminds me of a boy running away.

"It's been a long time," she continues, without expecting an answer. "But what can you do? You will always be my boys. Many of you still come to see me. The ones who stayed up north and the ones who came back here."

My mind slowly filters the information, like an image reacting to chemical agents and gradually developing on the satin-finish paper of a photograph. Mouth, hair, eyes, the outline of her cheekbones. But, above all, her voice. The voice that sang through a megaphone as the train pulled out of the station, the voice that rebuked me for not picking up Derna's letters.

It has started raining again, but it is a mere sprinkle, so feeble it hardly lands on the ground before it evaporates in the heat. The three of us are the only ones left standing in front of the church.

43

THE FRUIT AND VEGETABLE STALLS AT THE Pignasecca market seem to be talking on their own. It is as if the shouts are coming directly from the food, from the piled-up baskets and wooden crates that are as colorfully displayed as works of art, rather than from the vendors. Maddalena walks in front of me, holding the boy's hand, while I lag behind, just as I used to do with you. You would always yell at me, but it wasn't my fault. It's not my fault, even now. It's the shoes that are hurting me. Every step I take rubs the blisters on my heel, until they burst again. As we cross the narrow street, crammed with produce and people, Maddalena turns to speak to me, then to the boy, then back to me. It's as if she always knows where to take us; me, the boy with the black hair, all the kids on the train. So we simply follow her.

Passersby push and shove their way through the crowds, and I no longer try to avoid them. Maddalena still wears pants, as she always did. In the darkness of the church, she looked as tall and strong to me as she did when I was a child. Now, however, in the complex grid of this neighborhood, age seems to have made her smaller and more fragile. The crowd is noisy, the air heavy. I instinctively plug my ears with my fingers in order to shut out the cacophony and attempt to isolate Maddalena's voice.

"The boy is called Carmine," she tells me. "He's your brother Agostino's son."

WHEN I WAS ABOUT TO TURN TEN, YOU WROTE TO US to say you were coming to Modena to give me a present, a surprise I would never have been able to imagine. It was the first time you had ever said you would come to see me, and we were all excited, including Rosa and Alcide. Instead, that morning you called, Derna answered the phone. You wished me a happy birthday and said that you were not coming anymore. The doctor had advised you to rest and not to travel. At the end of the phone call, you said, "Will you come to see your baby brother when he is born?" I didn't answer. Tears were burning my eyes, as if I was running a high fever.

A few months later, the news arrived. You had had another boy and had called him Agostino, like your father, bless his soul. His last name was Speranza, like all your children, who were so full of hope. I decided there and then I would never come to your house again.

Not long after, I asked Alcide if I could try for the Conservatory. He paid for my train ticket and for a new jacket, but I was the one that had to earn the place at the music school. One morning that fall, my teacher, Maestro Serafini, accompanied me all the way to Pesaro. I stared through the window as a thick layer of fog buried the Po Valley under a shroud. "Here I am again," I thought to myself. The regular cadence of train wheels clacking on tracks was taking me far away from my home.

We walked into a room with dark wooden floors and red velvet armchairs, where other kids my age were sitting. Maestro Serafini left me there to wait for my audition. When my turn came, I took my violin out of its case and started playing: my left hand on the strings, my right hand on the bow. It was my first ever audition; I had chosen an aria from Pergolesi's *Stabat Mater*. I was accepted, with a scholarship that included my room and board.

44

MADDALENA STOPS AND WHISPERS IN MY EAR that the boy's mother and father have had a run-in with the law.

"What do you mean?" I ask her.

"They're in jail," she says, still whispering, so the boy doesn't hear.

I stop in the middle of the street, as kids riding three-up on a white scooter brush past my elbow. Maddalena and the boy vanish in the throng, and I start running. I finally reach them, just as Maddalena is unlocking her front door.

"Here we go," she says.

We walk up two floors until we reach an apartment with "Criscuolo" written beside the doorbell. Maddalena's house is tiny and extremely tidy. It looks like a temporary residence; somewhere she stays a few months before moving on. And yet she has lived here for more than thirty years, she tells me. She doesn't like having too many things around, only what she really needs. Hardly anything, I think.

Maddalena sits us down in her kitchen and pours two glasses of iced water.

"Would you like some Idrolitina in there? I can do it right away."

Idrolitina! From the bottomless well of long-lost memories, out pops Idrolitina. Sitting at another kitchen table, a glass bottle filled with water from the faucet, the yellow sachet of sodium salts held between my thumb and index finger. I would shake the sachet, rip the corner off, and it was my special treat to pour the magic soda powder into the bottle, put the top on, and shake the bottle hard.

I follow the same routine now, fifty years later, as if it's a piece of music I know by heart, and then I take the top off and pour the sparkling water into three cups.

"Carmine," Maddalena says. "Do you like crayons?"

The boy doesn't answer. Maddalena hands him a blank sheet of paper and a few colored crayons.

"Draw me a nice picture, will you? A portrait. But make me look nice, okay? Draw me nice and young, like when I first met your uncle Amerigo. Here, take a look."

She places an old black-and-white photo in front of the boy, and I catch a glimpse of her as I once knew her.

A little perplexed, he starts drawing. Maddalena and I go into the other room, a living room with two armchairs, and a coffee table between them. There's no TV; just a radio. We sit facing each other: two people with the main part of their lives behind them and, to varying degrees, only the margins to look forward to.

"I've seen lots of the kids who went north on those trains, like you did. They wanted me to write letters for them, and their parents asked me to send a note to those people they didn't even know, who had taken care of their kids for six months, a year, or more. Many stayed in touch. The families took their summer or winter vacations together. They went on helping, even from afar."

I gaze at the photos on the wall. In one, boys in shorts and girls in little dresses are waving diminutive Italian flags. The photo is black and white, veering toward sepia, but the flags stand out against the gray faces in bright red, white, and green. In another, the kids are at the station in Bologna after a night on the train. Their clothes are crumpled, their faces gaunt. But some of them are laughing in the midst of all the chaos. Two women are holding up a banner, which says, "We are the Mezzogiorno kids. Emilian solidarity and love show there is no north or south in this country, there is just Italy." The sentiment shows its age, I think. What outdated, unfashionable words they are.

"We helped so many kids, but it's a never-ending task," Maddalena goes on. "Your nephew, Carmine, was staying with his grandmother; Don Salvatore, the priest, helped out a little, too. Now he's on his own."

"I didn't know anything about Agostino. When did this happen?"

"A few months ago, but don't ask me anything else. I kept in touch with Antonietta, but she never told me anything about your brother's affairs. She said he was innocent, and that he would prove that he and his wife had done nothing wrong. They'd been framed. I'd heard he was in with the wrong people, and he'd made a lot of money. The charge must be serious, as they didn't even let him attend his mother's funeral. Carmine was always on his own, even before the arrest. If it hadn't been for his grandmother . . . Now the social services will start meddling."

I look at the boy through the living room door, kneeling on the chair, his elbows leaning on the table. I look for a resemblance to you, or to his father, Agostino, the good son, the one who stayed close by. His hair is black and straight, just like yours.

"He's a good kid, though he goes off the rails every now and again," Maddalena says. "What about you? Are you married? Kids?"

The boy in the kitchen picks up another sheet of paper and turns to look at me. Our gazes meet for a few seconds, then I look away, focusing again on the photographs on the wall.

"Yes, I'm married," I lie, again. She nods and smiles, encouraging me to invent an alternative life for myself with two grown-up kids who study music. Then I change the subject, because lying to her is hard.

"Do you remember Tommasino?"

She hands me a glass of homemade *limoncello*.

The curly dark-haired boy suddenly appears on the wall of my memory, like one of the black-and-white pictures in this room.

"Are you still in touch?"

"I'm not in touch with anybody," I tell her. "I didn't even know what Agostino was up to, how old his son was, that he had ended up in jail, that my mother had a bad heart . . ." I realize I'm raising my voice, so I stop talking and avoid her eyes. Then I shrug, with a sigh. For Maddalena the past doesn't matter. Even though she's old now, all she cares about is what she can still do. In this respect, she hasn't changed.

"Tommasino has had a great career. With the help of his babbo up north he was able to go to law school, even though he came back here to live with his family. He went on to become a judge."

"Really? The boy who used to steal apples from Capajanca's cart at Piazza del Mercato and run away with his haul . . ."

"Maybe that's exactly why," Maddalena says. "He works with kids. He works in the juvenile courts, with probations. He's helped me out a few times. I was an elementary school teacher for years in a neighborhood where many of the kids' parents were either in jail or at large . . . whenever I needed help, or advice, I would always ask him."

Maddalena pauses, makes an anguished face, leans over to check on the boy in the kitchen, takes another sip of the sweet yellow liqueur, and then starts again.

"It was easier in the old days. There used to be the Party, there were the comrades, the men and women who were fellow cardholders. There's nothing left now. If you want to do something good, you need to do it on your own, with no support from anyone else. There used to be Party cells, which organized activities for children, neighborhood by neighborhood, keeping them off the streets. Now only the church is helping . . . I'm not against it, the priests do no harm. In fact, they often do a lot of good. But it's not politics. I don't know whether I'm saying this right. What I mean is, it's charity, and that's different."

"History moves on; things change," I say.

"History moves on, but some things should stay the same. The idea of solidarity. Do you remember? Sol-i-dar-i-ty . . ."

"What about the blond Communist? The one who was flirting with you."

"Who, Guido? Flirting with me? We were all comrades at the time. We were involved in so much stuff, we didn't think about love at all. At least, I didn't."

"Maybe you didn't, but he did . . . I remember how he looked at you the day we left. When I saw him up at Party headquarters, he looked like a tortured soul. He was arguing with two or three other men, then, when he saw you, he was completely transformed . . ."

"Poor Guido!" Maddalena sighed. "He was expelled from the Party in the end. A sad story. He went to live in another city and abandoned politics altogether. Then he became a college professor, but something inside him was broken. He was never the same again. With me, too. We were fond of each other, not like you mean, but we liked each other. Anyway, we had lost our connection."

Maddalena shakes her head, and a lock of silver-white hair falls over her eyes.

"Well, it wasn't all good, to be honest," she continues. "It was great, because I was twenty years old and because I was in love with the idea. But there were bad things, too. There were some people who were in love with themselves and nothing else. Ideals took second place. Or came last."

Maddalena reaches out across the coffee table and takes my hand. There are brown liver spots on the back of hers and on her fingers.

"You know about all this. You were helped, you studied, you became a revered musician, you had opportunities. You are a respectable gentleman now, and you appreciate that it is worth it, being active in society is worth it, even though it is never enough, and it is never completely right. Whatever we *can* do, we *must* do."

I take my hand out of her clasp and sit there in silence. A revered musician, a respectable gentleman. I'm not sure I recognize myself in Maddalena's description.

"Maddalena, I understand what you are saying, and I am flattered, believe me. But my life is what it is. I am what I am. I'm over fifty. You chose not to have kids of your own and to look after other people's; I chose to devote my life to music. We all make our own choices. The kid has a father already. I had to go and find myself one."

Maddalena looks at me with a new face, one that is not inscribed in my memories.

"You don't get to choose everything. Some choices are forced on you by others . . ."

"Why are you telling me this, Maddalena? You are talking to a boy who was put on a train at the age of seven . . . On one side, there was my mother. On the other, everything I ever wanted: a family, a home, a room of my own, warm food, my violin. A man willing to give me his name. I was helped. A great deal, it's true. But I was also terribly ashamed. Hospitality, solidarity, as you say, leaves a bitter taste behind on both sides. Those who give, and those who receive. That's why it's so difficult. I dreamed of being like everyone else. I wanted them to forget where I came from and why. I gained a lot, but I paid the full price for it and I gave up a lot, too. Imagine, I've never told anyone my story."

"I haven't told anyone my story, either. Who do you take me for?"

Maddalena glares at me. For a second, I have no idea why, Zandragliona's story flashes through my mind; the one where Teresinella was shooting from the terrace, her whole body shaking with every shot.

"I had gotten pregnant when I was seventeen. The father was a kid like me and didn't want to know. They took me to an aunt's in the countryside for the whole pregnancy. My father was scared of being expelled from the Party if anyone found out. After the baby was born, they took her away. They took her away in secret, without telling me. I woke up one morning, bursting with milk, and she wasn't there."

Teresinella's body when she stops shooting and stops shaking;

Maddalena's eyes looking for her baby girl and not finding her. Her words register incredibly slowly, as if their function is to retrace her whole life, from the morning she woke up with her breasts engorged to this moment, and to stretch out time in order to close the gap of all the years that have gone by.

Maddalena starts smiling again, as if it's an old habit she can't avoid, and I recognize her once again.

"What I couldn't do for her," she declares, "I did for others."

45

MADDALENA WALKS ME TO THE DOOR. THE boy follows her, clinging to her side, his hands behind his back. I try to avoid his eyes. Maddalena suddenly brings her hand to her forehead and rolls her eyes. She says she was about to forget something important. She leaves the boy and me alone in the narrow entrance for a few minutes. I'm tired and eager to get back to my hotel. I can't stop thinking about the little body stolen from her mother.

The boy and I exchange looks, listening to the sounds coming from the living room, without speaking. Then the boy pulls his hand out from behind his back and produces the two sheets of paper. On one, there's his portrait of Maddalena as a young woman; on the other, there's me. I take it and look at it. He has drawn a pink oval with two little blue circles in it, reddish hair, and a downward-curving red mouth. I look at it, puzzled.

"It's you," he says. "I made you younger, too, is that okay?"

I look at it close up, and then from a distance, pretending to observe it in great detail to appreciate all its features. I don't know what the boy expects of me. I hazard a comment.

"Why have I got a parrot on my shoulder?"

"What parrot? That's your violin; Nonna Antonietta said you'd had it since you were a kid."

The scene of me looking under the bed and finding nothing flashes before my eyes. The boy watches me closely. Maybe he wants me to tell him the story. Kids always want stories. But I don't know how to tell this one. I fold the picture and put it in my pocket.

"Thank you" is all I say.

The boy shrugs and acts superior, as if he has given me a great gift and received nothing in exchange.

"I know a lot about you," the boy says slyly. "My nonna told me."

"Did Nonna talk to you about me?"

"She kept all the newspaper cuttings about you."

"That's not true. She's never even heard me play."

"Once we saw you on TV. She bought the set specially so she could see you." He looks at me, gauging the effect of his words. "You're famous."

"Do you like that I'm famous?"

The boy shrugs again, and curls up his mouth. I'm unable to decipher his answer.

"Will you teach me one day?"

"What do you want me to teach you?"

"To be famous."

"Okay . . . we'll see . . ."

"Then I can go on TV, too."

"Maddalena, I need to get going . . ."

"Here we go!" Maddalena returns with a yellowing photograph and places it on the table. "Here it is! I was sure it was here. Yessir . . . !"

The photo was taken in front of the Reclusorio, the hospice for the poor. Maddalena is in the center, with a few other young women her age. Next to her are the blond Communist and Comrade Maurizio, who later became mayor.

Surrounding them is a group of children, some with their mothers, others without. Maddalena touches all the faces that time has meanwhile transformed, some of them unrecognizably. Her thin fingers, with their close-cut, clean nails, trace the rows of faces one by one, as if she were reading, until they finally pause on a face. A little boy with big eyes that look gray in the black-and-white photo, standing next to his mother, who is young and beautiful, with high cheekbones and long, raven-black hair, braided and pinned up. Her lips are fleshy but deadly serious; they do not part in a smile. You can see she didn't know what to do with her hands, out of embarrassment at being photographed, so she had put one hand on the boy's shoulder. In fact, the boy was turning to look at her, surprised by the unfamiliar gesture.

I look at myself in the photo. Then I look at you. We are both standing there, both looking unsettled, just before we are separated.

"Remember to go and say 'hi' to Tommasino before you leave," Maddalena says at the door when I finally manage to get out onto the stairs. I don't answer her, but I do turn around one last time because I know I'll never see her again and I am overtaken by a feeling of anticipation of nostalgia. The boy's head appears from behind her. He doesn't say anything; he just looks at me with a disappointed expression on his face, as if I'm an imposter; someone who has failed to keep their side of the bargain. What was this boy expecting from me? And what could I do for him, in any case? Money, gifts, a letter every now and again? I remember all the times I hadn't kept my side of the bargain and had found it easier to run away, rather than live up to the promise.

46

I WALK BACK DOWN THE SAME STREET THE THREE of us came up on. The market sellers have taken down their makeshift stalls, and the street looks twice as wide as before. It is also less sweltering. A cool breeze, carrying the scent of the sea, is picking up, a reminder that the sea is close by even when it is out of sight.

I don't feel like going back to my hotel. I'm not hungry, either. I can't tell whether I miss you and I haven't yet worked out what form missing you will take. We have gotten used to missing each other; all these years have been a series of missed appointments. As if, from the moment you put me on that train, we had traveled along two different tracks, which never crossed again. But now what is missing is irretrievable, and I know I will never meet you again. I worry that our whole life has been a mix-up, a miscommunication between you and me. A love made up of misunderstandings.

There's not a soul left on the street; an unnatural silence has fallen. All I can hear are the out-of-tune blasts of a stadium horn in the distance and a few firecrackers going off. The storekeepers on Via Toledo are hastily rolling down their shutters, so that they can rush home and watch the match. I take one of the narrow streets back up into the Spanish Quarter. Halfway up, on the right, there's a cobbler's workshop. He's not closing, and he's in no hurry. He sits in the small, dark cavern, piled high with shoes that need repairing or resoling. I peer inside and realize I could ask the old man behind the counter whether he might be able to help me, given that my shoes are still hurting. The old man tells me to sit down on a stool and take my shoes off. I do as he says, sitting in my socks and looking around. The cobbler picks my shoes up one at a time, inspects them from every possible angle, and then looks at my feet. I wiggle my toes inside my socks, as if they're wild animals in a cage. Without saying a word, signaling to me to wait, he disappears into a back room. He returns with an object in his hand in the shape of a wooden foot attached to a handle with a big black screw. I watch the old man with bated breath, as if he were about to cast a magic spell. He slips the stretcher into my right shoe and cranks the handle once, twice, three times. Then he pulls it out and repeats the same operation with the left shoe. Last, he dips his brush in shoe wax, polishes the shoes to a mirror shine, and puts them down in front of me. I look at him as if to say, "Is that it?" The old man stands there, waiting for me to put my shoes back on. When I stand up, the shoes are no longer rubbing against my heels. I take a step, and then another. It's unbelievable. The old man, who hasn't said a word all this time, finally speaks.

"All feet are different, every single one has its own shape. You need to indulge your feet, otherwise all of life is suffering."

I thank him and ask how much it is.

"Nothing, it was a cinch," the cobbler answers, waving his hand in the air and disappearing back into his cavern. I start walking back to my hotel, my step springier, my head higher. Anyone who saw me walk by right now would think I was a man without a care in the world.

47

WHEN I OPEN MY EYES, IT IS STILL DARK. I toss and turn in my bed, but I am unable to get back to sleep. So I get up and go out onto the balcony. I look out at the horizon and see the first hint of light in the sky. I never liked dawn. Dawn makes me think of restless nights, unsettling dreams, emergencies, early morning flights to foreign cities. For me, every city is foreign.

I go into the shower and stay under the spray for a long time. Then I get dressed in light pants and a white shirt, with no jacket. I put my socks and shoes on, taking the Band-Aids from my bedside table, and then putting them back again. I go back into the bathroom and look at myself in the mirror. I stand there staring at my reflection, as if I'm seeing it for the first time. The eyes are the same. They have never changed. That deep blue, which came from who knows where? Maybe from that mysterious father, enamored of America, who left me nothing but my name, and then promptly ran away. Your eyes were black, like your hair and your eyebrows, which were delicate and distinct, almost as if they had been drawn with charcoal. I was just a child, but I knew you were beautiful. Not beautiful in a way a boy would see his mother. I had a feeling that men liked you. I could feel their eyes on you as you walked by, and I could hear their words loaded with innuendo. When I was born, you were so young. You had lost both your parents: your father in action and your mother under an air raid. You survived, and were left all on your own. You started taking in sewing in order to get by; a little mending here, a little repairing there. You never wanted to ask anybody for help. The men in your life left you nothing but children. What have you left me? What do I have left of you? Perhaps your way of looking askance at life, always a little suspicious of the hidden catch. And that taciturn air. I was such a chatterbox as a child, but now, in my maturity, now that I am twice the age you were then, I have ended up resembling you. Talking is no longer my strong point. The childhood ingenuousness has turned into a mask of cynicism, and the frankness has become an ease with lying.

The hotel breakfast is not being served yet, so I decide to go to the café. There's time. It is still early. I walk along the seafront to Piazza del Plebiscito. I feel less like a tourist today, but not yet a native of the city. Maybe this is my fate: always to be someone who has returned.

I stop at a cake shop on Via Toledo that hasn't changed since my day. It is exactly as I remember it, with shelves the color of sugar paper in the windows, the steady stream of sfogliatella pastries coming out of the ovens in the back room, filling the sidewalk with the fragrance of vanilla and wildflowers. The man behind the counter is old, his eyes an indefinite color, as if they had faded over the years; the little gray hair he has left combed back with pomade. I desperately try to tether that face, those eyes, that way of talking, to my memories. It was here that Tommasino and I used to come with the few lire we could get from Pachiochia and share one pastry, as if it was the most extraordinary thing in the world. Before I left, so many things seemed exceptional.

I sit at a table, lapped by a single ray of sun, and enjoy my pastry. I could be another person right now: an accountant, an office worker, a shoe repairer, a doctor. I pay the bill and set off on foot.

The juvenile court is a squat red building with a gray fence around it up in the hilly area of the city. I ask the doorman, who is short, and with a single strand of hair combed over his pate, where Justice Saporino's office is.

"Justice Saporino . . ." the doorman repeats, stroking his almost bald head. "He receives only by appointment. Do you have an appointment?"

"I don't need an appointment," I say, unexpectedly recovering some of the bravado of my youth. "Just tell him my name: Amerigo Speranza."

The small man is dubious. He would like to send me away, but suspects I may be someone important he hasn't recognized. Unwilling to be held responsible, he picks up the phone and dials the required number, just in case. The phone rings a few times before a voice answers. The doorman says my name and holds on for a few seconds. Long enough for the judge's memory on the other end of the phone to conjure up an image of me and him, when we were at least two feet shorter and our hair was a different color.

"You can go up, third floor," the short man with the comb-over says, sincerely incredulous.

I walk quickly over to the elevator, while the doorman leans out of his glass booth, trying to work out who he was dealing with.

When Tommasino opens the door and finds me standing there in front of him, we can read the time that has gone by in our eyes. There is no need to synchronize the past with the present. It is as though the years that have stood between my escape on the train and his opening this door had simply never existed, as if they were a momentary hiatus between two contiguous or extremely close events. A parenthesis filled with things for both of us, good and bad; a lifetime's parenthesis that is irrelevant in the story of our friendship.

Tommasino's office is cramped, but well organized. He shows me the photo of his wife and two children, a boy and a girl, who are now both in their thirties. They are both good kids, he tells me. The boy had gone to law school, but soon realized cooking was his passion and opened a restaurant in the Vomero quarter; the girl had become a teacher, but was currently on maternity leave. News of his children, more than anything else, makes me falter and recalculate the distance that lies between us after all these years. When he shows me a picture of his granddaughter, I understand that there is a crevasse across the time that separates us. Our lives have gotten out of sync.

Tommasino runs his hands through his hair, which is still dark and curly, with a few flecks of gray, and combed back. We're both over fifty, but I feel as though I have aged worse than him, more in a hurry.

"Carmine has suffered a great deal. I don't mean like us; things are different now. But if there were still those trains, our trains..."

Tommasino is not ashamed of our story. He looks around his office, and I can see that the little gray room stuffed with files fills him with pride. I look at my hands, the calluses on my fingertips, and I feel as though I have made it to adulthood with no purpose.

"Amerì," Tommasino continues. "Think about it. You're the only family he has left."

I sit in silence. I don't want to answer. I don't even know what the question is. Tommasino looks at me with the same face as the boy's yesterday when I left Maddalena's house, as if I hadn't kept a promise. I've never promised anyone anything. I preferred to be alone rather than make promises. In order to avoid his gaze, I observe all the details in his office: the books lined up on the shelves, the desk in light wood, the chair with the shape of his back imprinted on it from all those years working here. On his desk, in a frame next to the one of his wife and children, and another of Donna Armida and Don Gioacchino, I see a photo of his babbo up north, his hair and mustache a little more salt than pepper, and of the wife, with her still impressive breasts and a few more wrinkles on her face. There is the answer. It's right in front of my eyes.

48

R ATHER THAN GO BACK TO THE HOTEL, I DECIDE to wander around the narrow streets of your neighborhood and say goodbye to them for the last time. The streets that felt oppressive and heavy when I first arrived now seem familiar. I am still scared of the past but, if anything, I'm going hunting for it.

This evening, your street is silent. I feel like I'm the only person left in the whole city. Before reaching the end of the street, I stop in front of a ground-floor apartment emanating the bluish light of a television. The shutters are open. Two chairs have been placed outside the door. It's Zandragliona's old apartment.

I wait there awhile, as if expecting to see her popping out at any minute with her apron tied around her waist and a wide-open smile on her face. Instead, a man's voice calls out to me.

"Are you looking for anyone in particular?"

An old man, with thin gray hair tied into a mangy pigtail that hangs down over his shirt collar, stands at the door.

"Who are you looking for?"

"Nobody, nobody. Sorry for the intrusion; good night."

The man shuffles out of the tiny apartment, dragging his feet. His eyebrows are bushy and bristly, and his eyes are an intense blue. He looks at me, blinking nervously. I turn back and stop in front of him. It is the old man from the church.

"Didn't Zandragliona live here once?" I ask, finally.

"Peace be with her soul . . ." the man says, rolling his eyes up toward heaven. "She died . . . well, it must be four years ago now," he continues, counting to four on his fingers and blowing out smoke rings as he does so. "Right after Gorbachev died . . ."

"Wait a minute," I say. "Gorbachev is still alive."

"Nossir," the old man insists. "Zandragliona told me in these precise words that Gorbachev was dead, communism was dead, and she didn't feel very well either. And then, a few days later, she died . . ."

I look at him to see whether he's joking, but he doesn't seem to be. He goes on producing smoke rings and carrying on with his story.

"I'm a widower, and I was living with my married daughter, her husband, and her children: two girls and one boy. Zandragliona didn't have any family, so after a few months, when nobody had claimed the property, I moved into the apartment. Are you family?" he asks, quite concerned, thinking he is about to lose his home.

"Don't worry. I have no claim whatsoever."

"You must be a journalist, then. Your face is familiar."

"No, I do commercials for aftershave."

The old man stands there without saying anything, blinking at intervals that appear to be regular. He lights another cigarette and blows a few more smoke rings that circle in the air. Finally, I get it.

"You're Capa 'e Fierro, aren't you?" I ask.

He doesn't answer, but he shifts to one side of the door.

"Trasìte!" he says, inviting me in, and controlling his impulse to blink long enough for me to see his old expression, his eyes the same blue as before. I stay on the threshold, uncertain. Then I stoop and go in. I can see the whole place in one sweep: the wallpaper, yellowing in the corners, but the same as before, the gray tones of the floor, the irregular, chipped tiles around the perimeter of the room. In the corner, in front of the bathroom door, I see what I think might be my special tile.

"Being that you are so kind . . ." I say to the man, who is lurking in a corner, lighting another cigarette, "I'd like to look for something that belongs to me, if you don't mind. May I?"

The man looks around him and opens his arms wide as if to ask what could possibly be of any interest in this place. Or perhaps to signify "go ahead" . . . I roll my sleeves up and kneel on the floor near the row of tiles next to the bathroom. I crouch with the same familiarity children have with the ground, the street, the floor. "Amerì, get up off of the floor," you would always scold.

I skim the tiles, stale dust under my fingertips. The pads of my fingers caress every square, feeling for irregularities. In the end, I focus on one tile that feels more worn out than the others. I stick my nails into the space between the tiles and pull, gently at first and then harder, but it won't budge. The old man observes me in silence, every now and again screwing up his eyes in an involuntary spasm. I feel as though he is studying my every gesture, but he may just be worried about his floor. At that very moment, the tile comes loose and I fall over backwards with the ceramic square still in my hand. Underneath, there's the hole.

"How do you know me?" the old man says as I survey the floor tiles.

I remember the packages hidden under our bed, the rags I

collected for you every day that we cleaned and mended and took to Capa 'e Fierro, so he could sell them. You and him locked up in our apartment with work to do, you used to say. Both of you sending me away.

"I kept a stall at the market when I was a kid, like you," I said.

The old man has stopped talking. I can't tell whether he's angry that I've wrecked his floor or just curious about what's down there. He's probably thinking about that money Zandragliona was supposed to have squirreled away. Or maybe he's going back down the same memory lane I am, trying to reconstruct the face of that redhead out of this middle-aged man.

I turn the other way, dig down into the hole with my arm, and take out a tin box with rusty corners. Under the layer of dust, you can still see the blue enamel and the trademark of the cookies it once held. Not that I had eaten them; the box was a gift to you from the deli on Via Foria. You used it for your sewing kit, but then it was Capa 'e Fierro himself who gave you a professional box made of wood, with twin lids and two expandable sections that opened upward, and lots of little compartments for all the different-colored cotton reels and the various-sized needles. The new wooden sewing box had three trays that could be lifted on metal hinges. It was so beautiful! To me, it looked like a spaceship from the science fiction comics on the shelves at the newsagents on the Corso. That was why you gave the cookie tin to me. You had never given me a present before, and that powder blue tin felt unique and precious. I never let anyone play with it, not even Tommasino. Zandragliona was the only person I showed it to, and we decided together to put everything I wanted to save inside, as if it were a strongbox. Zandragliona told me she had a secret place, and that's where my treasures have been preserved all this time and where they would have stayed if this old man with his bewildered expression hadn't invited me in. They would have outlived Zandragliona and even me. Like everything that is suspended, postponed until the next day without knowing you are about to die, without knowing that the next day is a day that will never come. Like your *pasta alla genovese*. Capa 'e Fierro and I stare at the tin box. Neither of us is in a hurry. Time has stretched out for both of us. All of a sudden, it has become comfortable, like my shoes. I place the tin on the brown Formica table without saying a word. Then I put my nails into the groove under the lid until it pops up with a metallic ring. One by one, my treasures reemerge onto Zandragliona's table, and with them, perfectly preserved, my capacity for recall.

The wooden top with string wound around it and a metal tip . . .

Ameri, do what Mamma says and stop that spinning, for the love of God!

The American beer bottle tops that a black, black soldier gave me . . .

Wuz ior neim, liddel boi? Wuz ior neim?

A piece of dry bread that Tommasino and I had swiped from Pachiochia's house . . .

Get out of here, you're a darn-right thief, you. You're no better than a rat, stealing bread like that!

Pieces of string, a walnut-shell boat with a tiny sail, a half-burned candle, a safety pin, a parrot feather that I picked up who knows where. Four objects that were already old or damaged when I first found them in some corner of some street somewhere. They were all the toys I had.

And then there were two yellowed pieces of paper folded in four, the corners consumed by mold. I unfold them, scared they will disintegrate right before my eyes. One is a newspaper cutting of a complete stranger, a tall man with curly hair I always imagined was red, with the caption below in block letters: GIGGINO 'O 'MERICANO. I had kept it so that I could fantasize about a father.

Capa 'e Fierro has been gaping at the relics as I take them out of the tin one by one. Then he abruptly drops to his knees. He's so skeletal that I worry he'll break. We are inches apart, and, for an instant, I think he wants to pet me. Instead, with a grunt, he sticks his arm into the hole so far that his ear is touching the floor. He would climb right down into the pit if it meant unearthing Zandragliona's famous supplies of money, jewels, gemstones, and gold. But he finds nothing. The only treasure is mine.

"It's not true you do commercials for aftershave," he says, with the air of a challenge.

I put the tin under my arm, wave goodbye, and head toward the door.

"Come and see me every now and again," the old man says as I leave, suddenly adopting the familiar *tu* form as if he were superior to me. "There are a lot of things I could tell you . . ." I hear him calling out when I am already out on the street. After he has closed the door, I stop a few yards from his window. From the shadows, I can see him blowing smoke rings up to the ceiling and then, certain he is not being watched, sticking his hand back down the hole. I go back to the front door of the apartment and see a white sticky label on the mailbox with a name written in pen: Luigi Amerio. In this city, everyone adopts a nickname, which they use all their life and even have printed on their death notices, otherwise people wouldn't know who they were. I never knew that Capa 'e Fierro's real name was Luigi Amerio.

In his first and last name, Capa 'e Fierro bears the names of both your children, Luigi and Amerigo. Or was it us that bore his name without our knowledge?

49

M ADDALENA TOLD ME YOU WERE CALLED Speranza, like me."

"I'm called Benvenuti. I was adopted."

"Am I going to be adopted now?"

Carmine trots by my side and never stops talking. You told me that I, too, used to ask a lot of questions when I was a kid. I was like quicksilver. What was it you called me? Ah, yes. A punishment from God!

"Mamma says that when I walk in the road, I have to hold an adult's hand," he says, trying to catch hold of mine.

"We're on the sidewalk here. There are no cars."

He thinks about it and shakes his head. He's not convinced. When Maddalena called me at the hotel and asked me to take the kid for a walk, because she was busy, I realized it was a trap. She's as stubborn as ever; things have to go as she wants them. Her world has no one left behind. I think of the big hall in Bologna, and the shame I felt when all the other kids were picked, and nobody took my hand to lead me away.

"Is it true that when you were little you had another mother?"

We get to the end of the sidewalk.

"My father told me. Nonna never wanted to tell me the story."

The traffic lights turn green for pedestrians.

"Lucky you! I'd love another mother sometimes," he says, reaching out to hold my hand as we cross the road. I notice his eyes are welling with tears.

His hand is soft and cool to the touch. Carmine squeezes hard and dries his eyes with his other arm. Together, we get to the other side of the road.

We're on the sidewalk again, but he won't let go of my hand. I remember Derna's smell when she wrapped me up in her coat at the bus station before going to Modena. I'm scared. The hand that until now had only been good at moving the bow of a violin was now potentially a tool for giving consolation and strength. It's so powerful, I'm not sure I'm capable of exerting it. The hand holding the child's, all of a sudden, feels weak. It has made a promise it may not be able to keep.

"It's too hot to go to the zoo today. I'll take you back to Maddalena's."

"Can we go another day?"

I think about my flight back to Milan and my concert tour, and I don't answer.

"When you get back, there's a surprise for you."

We get to Maddalena's door. Retracing my steps back to the hotel, I feel the softness of his palm pressing into the middle of mine.

50

W HEN I GO BACK INTO THE JUVENILE COURT, the doorman with the comb-over lets me through on the spot. He even calls me sir. In your city, titles are not academic, they're honorary.

"Come this way, sir. Justice Saporito is expecting you," he says, walking with me to the elevator and pushing the button for me. Tommasino opens the door and then goes to sit behind his desk. I sit down, too.

"I came to say goodbye."

Tommasino combs his hair back with his hands as if he still had the rebellious curls he had when he was seven years old.

"Well, that's news. Last time, you ran away without saying anything!"

Then he looks over at me.

There's a knock at the door. Tommasino says to come in. The doorman's head comes around the door.

"Justice, would either of you like an expresso?"

In this city of ours, coffee is much more than a drink; it's an act of devotion. Tommasino waves his hand, and the doorman disappears behind the door.

"Do you remember the painted sewer rats?" I ask him as I stare at the photos on his desk.

Tommasino's serious expression cracks into a smile

"Who could ever forget it?"

"Before we left, anything was possible, even selling rats as hamsters. When we got back, I didn't believe anything anymore. The magic had gone out of me. There was nothing down here, just my mother. Everything else was up there. I chose everything else and became what I became: Maestro Benvenuti."

I stop, because I'm unsure how to go on. Then the words start flowing on their own, without my having to choose them.

"I'm still the other person, too. The one that has the same last name as Carmine."

I'm not sure Tommasino is following me. His life has been different. He's never had to choose. On his desk there isn't a single photograph missing.

"I thought I might take the boy," I blurt out. "I'm the only family he has left, as you said. Until things settle down a little, anyway. Until we know a little more . . ."

"That's a really nice offer, Amerì, but . . ."

"I know. I know it's complicated. I live on my own, I travel a lot, but I can do something for him. I have had good things happen to me, and I have never given anything back."

Tommasino opens his mouth to say something, but closes it again.

"I'm not saying forever; just for a few months. We'll leave together and then we'll see . . ."

"Amerì, there is no need now: the mother is out of jail."

"Ah . . ."

"She went home yesterday."

"Has she been cleared?"

"Not exactly. She's under house arrest, in consideration of the fact there is a juvenile. Anyway, they have dropped some of the charges against her."

"What about Agostino?"

"We don't know yet. They're preparing the case. We'll see. The indictment is serious."

"Drugs?"

Tommasino makes an apologetic face as if it were all our fault, mine and his in equal parts.

"And the boy? Are we sure he'll be okay? And the mother . . ."

"I don't know. I'm not happy. The right thing to do isn't always the easiest. The mother is back, and that's a good thing, but it doesn't put a smile on my face."

"I'd like to see him before I go. I want to speak to him. I want to tell this woman that she can call me, that I can help them. Her, the boy, my brother. Do you have their address?"

Tommasino doesn't get it. Until a few days ago, it was them chasing me. Now it feels like the opposite. My hand has been shaken in a promise, and it has started making plans for the future. Tommasino pulls a file from the pile on his desk and leafs through the papers inside. Then he scribbles an address and a number on a scrap of yellow notepaper.

Tommasino and I say goodbye as if we would be seeing each other the next day, as two friends always say goodbye. I have only taken a few steps when he calls me back.

"Wait! There's something I want to give you."

He starts rummaging through his desk drawer and eventually finds the piece of paper folded in four.

"I went to look for this after you came to see me. You brought back so many memories . . ."

He unfolds the yellowing sheet, and the faces of three children sketched in pencil appear: the coal head, "evil hair," and the dirty, straw-haired tomboy.

"Those are the portraits that young man drew of us the day we left," I say.

"You keep it; it's a gift from me. He signed and dated it. Comrade Maurizio, remember?"

I say nothing. I fold the sheet back in four and look down at the toes of my shoes, still amazed they are not hurting. I rest a hand on the door handle and gaze out the window. The wind is bending the treetops in the direction of the sea. The weather is changing.

51

THERE IS A BRASS PLAQUE ON THE DARK WOODEN door: A. SPERANZA. It could be me. This could be my house, my life, but it's not. This is Agostino's apartment and his life. I don't know if it has been better or worse than mine. There's grass and then there are weeds. That's what you used to think. I stand in front of the door without knocking and try to conjure up the other Amerigo, the one who stayed in the city where he was born and lived there all his life. I can see him strolling through the narrow streets and alleys, different but the same. Made different by a different life. Fatter, perhaps. With less hair. A darker complexion. More smiley. With a woman at his side. A woman with black hair and big breasts. He would be a craftsman, or a factory worker. He would have gone to work with Mariuccia's father, the cobbler. That's what you wanted. Then, as he grew up, he would have opened a little shoe store. He would have resoled shoes and made them as good as new. He would have adapted them to the feet of those who had to wear them. Because he knew what it meant to wear shoes that did not belong. Or perhaps he would have made shoes himself; handcrafted ones. The shop might have done well or it might not have. It might even have been very successful. He would have exported his shoes abroad. To America. And he would have taken you there. He would have taken care of you.

THERE'S A BELL BUT I DON'T PUSH IT. I KNOCK GENTLY, with my knuckles.

"Who is it?" a woman's voice asks from inside.

"Amerigo. You don't know me. I came to say goodbye to the boy."

I can hear voices behind the door. The woman is talking to her son, who is in the other room watching TV. Then silence. I knock again and finally the door opens a chink, just enough for me to see a pair of hazel eyes set in a long, thin face framed by blond bangs.

"I'm sorry, sir," my sister-in-law says. "I can't let you in; I'm not allowed to let anyone in. Agostino has told me a lot about you."

"We're family, can we at least use first names?" I say, peering into the space between the door and the wall.

"My name's Rosaria," she says, reaching her hand out through the gap. "Listen, if you like, you could take Carmine out for a bit. I'm not allowed out of the house."

The boy slips through the opening and grabs my hand.

"Uncle!" he exclaims. His eyes are shining as if I had kept my promise, after all.

"I'll bring him back in an hour or so, don't worry," I say.

"I'm not worried," she answers.

She is about to close the door when she changes her mind.

"You're not to worry either," she says, her expression tense. Her face is still young and fresh; the bags under her eyes must be a recent addition. "Agostino is a good man. They've got it all wrong. We are all respectable people here."

"Of course," I answer, a little embarrassed. "I know."

"No, you don't know anything," she says, opening the chink a little wider. I can now see her hands resting on the doorjamb. Her fingers are long and tapered, her nails cut short, like a pianist's. "You don't know anything about us; you have never cared one bit."

As she is speaking, bringing her face closer to mine, so that she can be heard without shouting, I discover that her eyes are not hazel but dark green.

"I'm sorry, Rosaria," I say, as if the apologies I owe her are also for you, Mamma.

"There's nothing to be sorry about," Rosaria says, suddenly changing tone as if she's no longer angry, just sad. "When Agostino gets home, I'll have him call you. He's made mistakes with you, too." As she says this, she gives a shy half-smile. She closes the door before I have time to say anything.

"Shall we go?" he says.

We stroll through the tree-lined avenues of this residential quarter. It feels like we are in another city. The faces are a different color, the features less pronounced, the tone of voice lower, the air cooler.

"Have you always lived here?" I ask him.

"No, when I was little, we all lived with Nonna Antonietta. That's what they told me, anyhow. I can't remember. But I was always at her house even when we lived here. I slept and played there. I went to the oratory playground at Don Salvatore's church . . ."

"You also hung out with your friends making trouble . . ."

"Mamma's always a wreck."

"Mine was, too."

"That's not true! Nonna was cheerful."

Love is always filled with misunderstanding.

We walk toward the park.

"Would you like an ice cream?" I ask.

He shakes his head.

"You don't like ice cream?"

"I don't feel like it."

"What do you feel like?"

"I miss Nonna."

"Me, too."

We walk in silence for a while, until we reach the park gates. The boy pulls my hand.

"You're leaving again, aren't you?"

I can't face lying to him.

"I'm leaving tomorrow, but I'll be back soon."

"Well, we'd better go quickly then."

"To do what?"

"It's a secret just for you. A surprise from Nonna. She said that when you came, we would surprise you together, but now . . ."

I look at him, and for the first time since I met him, he smiles. I realize he has a gap in his front teeth. Here they say a tooth mouse takes your baby teeth away.

"Now I don't know if it's still a surprise."

"Let's see," I say.

We go up the hill again and take the Funicolare Centrale. We get to your neighborhood, with its low buildings, crammed tight together, and its railings draped with drying laundry, wedged-in between the more elegant streets, a stone's throw from the piazza where the theater is. In your street, people's voices take me back in time to when everyone was chanting, "Good *evening*, Donna Antonietta!" "Top of the *day* to you, Donna Pachiochia!" "How's the *little one* today?" "He's growing *so* fast, just like the weeds . . ." they would chant. "How's *business* today?" "I don't *understand*, Pachiochia . . ." "Well, *ask* Capa 'e Fierro . . ." "There are *too many* tongue waggers around!" "Is your *husband* coming back?" "*Of course* he is!" "*Ex-cuse me*, Donna Antonietta!" "Good *ni-ight*, Donna Pachiò."

WHEN WE GET TO YOUR DOOR, I TAKE CARMINE'S hand and squeeze it, just a little. The door is still on the latch. Nobody has touched anything. We go in together. I feel sadness in my stomach. The boy leads me to your bed.

"It's under here," he says.

I don't understand.

"It's here. Your surprise."

I crouch down on the floor and look under the bed, where once upon a time Capa 'e Fierro stored his contraband. I look at the boy. His lips are pressed tight, holding in his excitement. I'm excited, too. I stretch out my arm and touch it.

"Nonna took ages, but she finally found it. We wanted to give it to you next time you came down."

I pull out the dusty case and open it. The violin is even smaller than I remembered it, almost like a toy. It feels like I'm receiving it as a gift again, only this time it's from you. Inside the case there's still the label with my name on it: "Amerigo Speranza."

"See? You're a Speranza, too."

52

I'VE COME TO THE GRAVEYARD TO BRING YOU A flower. For the first time in many years, we are alone. Just you and me. At first, I tried praying, but I soon realized improvising was not a good idea under the circumstances. Then I tried talking to you. I thought I had important things to say to you, but nothing came to mind. I'd consumed so much rage that I'd forgotten why I was angry.

The sky is still. The weather is neither good nor bad; it's waiting to see what happens. A few people, mostly old, are looking for their loved ones along the rows of gravestones. They are carrying fresh flowers and oil for the grave lights. I've put my flower in front of your stone. I haven't set out any lights. I remember you didn't like going to sleep with the lights on. The flower will wither tomorrow or the day after. It doesn't matter. The memory of you will not lose its bloom; all the years I spent far away from you have turned into a long love letter. Every note I played, I played for you. There's not much else. I have nothing else to say. I don't need to know your answers now. About my father, about Agostino, about your distance, about my silence. My questions are still there. I'll keep them with me, take them around. They'll keep me company. I haven't resolved anything, but it doesn't matter anymore.

I stay for a while in front of my flower. I stand there until my legs start to ache. Then, and only then, I say goodbye.

The things we haven't said to each other, we'll never say now. For me, it was enough to know that you were on the other end of that railway line, all those miles away for all those years, with my coat clasped to your breast in a cross. That's where you will always be. Stay there. Wait. Don't go.

53

ALL OF A SUDDEN, IT'S COLD. IT'S JUNE, BUT IT could be November. It rained last night. A storm that felt like the end of the world. And yet this morning a wan sun came up: a thin, wrinkled thing, suspended in the gray sky. The temperature has dropped, though, an advance warning of fall. People on the street mutter that nothing is certain these days. They had had to get their coats out from the inside of the wardrobes where they had been stored for the coming winter.

Garibaldi Station is crowded. When we used to go with Tommasino to watch the departing trains, everything looked twice the size. I remember the speaker system announcing arrivals and departures, people hauling heavy suitcases onto their shoulders and making their way along the platforms. I look up at the display, read the numbers, and walk slowly to my platform. The last time I was here, it was dark. You and I had argued, and I'd run barefoot away from the singing and lights of the Piedigrotta Festival. Since then, I've always avoided train stations. They made me uncomfortable. But yesterday, I went to a travel agency and changed my plane ticket to a train ticket. I feel the need to take the same journey I took so many years ago.

A cold wind starts to blow. Everyone waiting on the platform wraps their coats around them more closely. I shiver in my linen jacket.

It has started to rain hard. I arrived in this city drenched in sweat and leave it soaked with rain. And yet I don't feel sad. The cheerfulness of the sun and the blue sky is a falsehood propagated by popular songs, while the dripping rain serves to remind me that time is passing and it is getting late.

I LOOK AT MY WATCH AND TURN AROUND ONE LAST time. I look over at the people huddling under the shelter and I sigh. The train pulls into the station with an out-of-tune whistle and screeches to a halt. I clamber slowly up the steps of the carriage, checking my ticket to see where my seat is. I don't sit down. I carry on staring at the platform shelter, waiting. A blond woman with a big suitcase bumps into me as she tries to maneuver her way past without asking permission. I'm about to tell her off rudely, but just at that moment I see them coming. Running against the wind, which is whipping up more strongly than before, hair flying, I see them go past my carriage and then stop a few yards ahead. The train gives another whooshing sound, but the doors are still open. I hurry out of the carriage. Carmine lets go of Maddalena's hand and runs toward me.

"The bus was late, there was traffic," he says, out of breath while I crouch down beside him. I don't say anything but I hold him tight.

"When I come back, I want to see you here waiting for me, okay?"

"Yes, Uncle," Carmine says. "I'll come with Papa."

The conductor gives a last whistle, and I go back on board. I put my head out the window, stretching my hand out, but I can't reach the boy's hand. I've given him my violin. The one you left for me. It's just the right size for him. Who knows whether he'll ever want to learn. He could do it right here, without needing to run away, without having to barter his dreams with everything he has.

Then the doors close, and the train starts moving. Maddalena and Carmine grow smaller and smaller, moving into the distance as the tracks slide under the carriage.

The city starts to recede, slowly at first, then faster, while tiny drops of rain bounce off the window at increasing speed. I sit in my seat and gaze outside: at the trees and houses running beside me, the tracks slipping past, the clouds.

A woman in a flowery dress sits opposite me. She opens a book and starts reading. She looks up from the pages every now and again, studying my face. Then she points at the violin case and smiles.

"Are you a musician? I'm a great fan of orchestral music."

"I'm a violinist."

"Did you come for a concert?"

"No, I came back to say hello to my family. I live in another city, but this is my home," I answer, surprised at how easy the truth is.

She reaches out her hand and introduces herself. I shake her hand and smile.

"Pleasure to meet you. Amerigo," I say, adding after a second, "Speranza."

The carriage is the perfect temperature; neither too hot nor too cold. The train glides silently. The voices around me hum and buzz. There's lots of time, and I'm in no hurry. I've already had the longest possible journey, retracing my steps all the way back to you, Mamma.

My violin is on the rack. The woman opposite is absorbed in her book. Every now and again our gazes meet. I suddenly feel exhausted, like a satisfied child who has everything he needs. I close my eyes, rest my head on the back of the seat, and succumb softly to sleep.

A NOTE ON THE LYRICS

The lyrics on pages 34, 68, and 165 are taken from the popular Socialist song "La Lega" (The League).

The lyrics on page 34 are taken from the song "Marcia Reale" (Royal March). Lyrics and music by Giuseppe Gabetti.

The lyrics on page 59 are taken from the popular Tuscan lullaby "Ninna Nanna, Ninna oh."

The lyrics on pages 68 and 91 are taken from the popular Italian song "Bella Ciao."

The lyrics on page 115 are taken from "Nessun Dorma" in the opera *Turandot*, libretto by Giuseppe Adami and Renato Simoni, music by Giacomo Puccini.

The lyrics on page 125 are taken from "Libiamo ne' lieti calici" in the opera *La Traviata*, libretto by Francesco Maria Piave, music by Giuseppe Verdi.

The lines on page 148 are taken from the popular Italian song "Bandiera Rossa" (Red Flag).

A NOTE FROM THE TRANSLATOR

The name of the central character of the novel, Amerigo (America) Speranza (Hope), signals a search of an identity. Is the father he never knew seeking his fortune in America, as his mother claimed? Hope is his only birthright; his name a talisman against bad luck. As with his shoe-counting game, Amerigo swings precariously between two different fates: spotting a pair of good shoes gives him the points for a star-studded prize, but he has never had any of his own to wear.

This novel was a challenge to translate, due to the complex forms of fracture embodied by Amerigo Speranza himself: of language (dialect versus Italian, as well as puns and wordplay), class and opportunity (post-war misery versus economic boom), politics (monarchists versus communists), space (south versus north), and time (child versus adult, 1940s Naples and Naples today). How much can the translator "carry across" from the original? A great deal, I hope—hope is our birthright as translators, after all, or we would give up before starting.

The first word in the novel—and in our own language development—is Mamma. In Amerigo's perception, her primal name is often mediated and emotionally distanced by referring to her as "Mamma Antonietta," a protective double that heralds the second mother to come. Nicknames in Naples represent another form of duality: replacing real names for a lifetime—even featuring in death notices—they evoke a personality trait that is often an antithesis. For example, "Zandraglia" comes either from the French *entrailles* (innards) or the Spanish *andrajo* (rags); in any case, it means "vulgar" or "stupid," whereas Zandragliona, Amerigo's neighbor and safe harbor was anything but that. "Pachiocchia" comes from the Italian *pacioccone,* meaning someone who is soft and easy-going, which the formidable monarchist in the novel is nothing of the kind. "Capa 'e Fierro" literally means "head of iron." *Capo* is also "boss" but the man who ran the rag trade turns out to be far less steely than Amerigo thought as a child. Returning as an adult, the name reels him back to his eternal quest for answers. Is Capa 'e Fierro the missing "head" Amerigo's heart has always longed for?

The train transporting poor southern kids immediately after the war to the plentiful and generous north literally "translates" them to a different reality. The dichotomy within Amerigo is compounded by his adoption: a new beginning, a new family, a new name, but at the same time an irreparable break with his past. Amerigo only realizes when he returns to Naples as an adult that the sounds of the city, especially the crowded alleyways of the Spanish Quarter where he grew up, have haunted him all his life–and overwhelm him on his return. The streets of Naples are ringing with music but Amerigo can only become a musician once he has left. "You can't eat music," his mother once reminded him. He is forced literally to swallow his talent in exchange for her love, which only reveals itself after her death when he tastes her leftover *pasta alla genovese.*

Ardone writes what can only be called a musical score for Naples, with the rising and falling cadences of the street conversations, market calls, or stress patterns of dialect which are represented on the page with marked divisions into syllables. Songs play an important role, too, and often symbolize a rupture. Amerigo dreads hearing the lullaby of his childhood, which tells the story of a baby being given away to a *uomo nero* (literally "black man," an atavistic "other"), and is relieved when his new mother, who has no experience of children, sings him the communist hymn, "Bella Ciao." An Italian will have known both songs intimately since childhood. At the same time, they will never have thought of the lullaby as menacing, just as we don't think of "Rock-a-bye Baby" falling out of the treetops as being scary.

It is the constant shift of perception from the familiar—linguistically and culturally—to the shadowy realm of the unfamiliar that makes Amerigo such an appealing character, both as a child and as an adult. Paradoxically, this allows readers in translation to follow the same dual trajectory, "carrying across" their own new meaning, hand in hand with Amerigo, crossing their fingers all the while, hoping against hope that he will make it to the other side.

—Clarissa Botsford

Here ends Viola Ardone's
The Children's Train.

The first edition of this book was printed and
bound at LSC Communications in
Harrisonburg, Virginia, October 2020.

A NOTE ON THE TYPE

The text of this novel was set in ITC Legacy Serif, a typeface designed by Ronald Arnholm in the early 1990s. Arnholm, then a graduate student at Yale, drew inspiration from Nicolas Jenson's (1420–1480) early Roman typefaces. ITC Legacy maintains the beauty and elegance of Jenson's original, while improving legibility with its open counters and clean character shapes.

An imprint dedicated to publishing international voices,
offering readers a chance to encounter other lives and other
points of view via the language of the imagination.